Gabriel stopped dead in his tracks.

He'd been expecting a woman in her late seventies. He'd known what she looked like. He'd had a photo of her emailed to him prior to this meeting.

Instead, he was looking at a young woman as slender as a reed, with silvery-white blond hair that tumbled in curls past her shoulders and down her back. Her skin was satin smooth and her eyes cornflower blue—as clear as crystal.

She was dressed in dungarees and one of the straps had slipped off her shoulder, revealing a cream vest underneath and the shadowy curve of a small breast.

He was annoyed at the sudden lapse of self-control, but even as he stifled it, he could still feel the stirring of his libido and the uninvited, utterly misplaced notion that this sort of immediate, knee-jerk physical reaction was just not him, and *that* annoyed him even more.

He abruptly broke the silence while moving forward.

"And you are?"

Secrets of the Stowe Family

Their next destination? True love!

When Max, Izzy and James's parents died in a tragic accident, all they had left was each other... Max, the oldest Stowe sibling, had to take charge, bring up his brother and sister—*and* take the helm of the family business.

Years later, their family business has been transformed into a global success! Still, there's more to life than just work, isn't there? It's time for the Stowe siblings to discover, as they travel the world, the business of love!

Meet the Stowe family in...

Max and Mia's story
Forbidden Hawaiian Nights

and

Izzy and Gabriel's story
Promoted to the Italian's Fiancée

Both available now!

Look out for James's story, coming soon!

Cathy Williams

PROMOTED TO THE ITALIAN'S FIANCÉE

Recycling programs
for this product may
not exist in your area.

ISBN-13: 978-1-335-40413-8

Promoted to the Italian's Fiancée

Copyright © 2021 by Cathy Williams

This edition published by arrangement with Harlequin Books S.A.

For questions and comments about the quality of this book,
please contact us at CustomerService@Harlequin.com.

Harlequin Enterprises ULC
22 Adelaide St. West, 40th Floor
Toronto, Ontario M5H 4E3, Canada
www.Harlequin.com

Printed in U.S.A.

Cathy Williams can remember reading Harlequin books as a teenager, and now that she is writing them, she remains an avid fan. For her, there is nothing like creating romantic stories and engaging plots, and each and every book is a new adventure. Cathy lives in London, and her three daughters—Charlotte, Olivia and Emma—have always been, and continue to be, the greatest inspirations in her life.

Books by Cathy Williams

Harlequin Presents

Visit the Author Profile page at Harlequin.com for more titles.

To my inspirational partner, David, and
my glorious daughters

CHAPTER ONE

'I'VE HAD A personal invitation.'

Evelyn Scott pushed the handwritten note across the kitchen table to Izzy. The salad the elderly woman had prepared earlier, using produce from the vegetable patch at the end of her garden, had been eaten, the home-made lemonade drunk and outside a burning orange sky signalled the arrival of dusk.

Here in Napa Valley, the horizons seemed limitless and the vast expanse of sky was a canvas upon which every shade of colour begged to be painted, depending on the time of the day and the vagaries of the weather. Izzy could have lain on her back in a field for hours, just appreciating its spectacular, ever-changing beauty.

'A personal invitation?' She reached forward to take the note and realised that, while they had been lazily conversing for the past hour and a half, while the older woman had listened and responded to everything Izzy had had to report, she had been busily hiding the fact that she was worried sick. And Izzy knew the source of that worry.

She read the note.

It was written on a piece of heavy, cream parchment paper, the sort of paper she associated with aggressive bankers calling in loans or hard-nosed lawyers threatening jail.

The writing confirmed that first impression. Long, determined strokes issued an invitation to tea, during which the sale of the cottage could be discussed 'face to face'. The invitation looked more like a summons.

'It's the first time I've been approached by the man himself.' Evelyn rose to her feet and began clearing the plates and glasses, waving aside Izzy's offer to help. 'You don't need to concern yourself with an old woman's problems. That's not why you came here in the first place.'

'Evelyn, your problem is my problem.'

It still felt weird after nearly a month to call the older woman 'Evelyn' instead of Nanny Scott, which was always how her mother had referred to her. To this day, Izzy had vivid memories of sitting in her mother's bedroom, watching as Beverley Stowe brushed her hair and dabbed on lipstick, smacking her lips together to distribute the colour evenly, inspecting her face from every angle as she chatted away. Izzy had listened avidly. She'd thought her mother to be the most beautiful woman in the world and she had drunk in every single thing that had passed her lips with the fervent adoration only a child was capable of.

There had been a thousand tales about Nanny Scott. Izzy had met Evelyn Scott for the first time on her one and only trip to California when she'd been nine, a year before her mum and dad had died in a plane crash. That holiday was etched in her mind because holidays with her parents had been few and far between. She could still relive the high-wire excitement of being with her parents for that heady, hot, lazy month in summer as though it had happened yesterday and not thirteen long years ago.

So now, sitting here, seeing the worry on Evelyn's face, Izzy felt anger surge inside her at the preposterous and intimidating antics of the billionaire who wanted to buy the cottage out from under the seventy-nine-year-old woman's feet, and to heck with what happened to her after that. He had sent his minions, but the message had not been delivered to his satisfaction, so here he was, knife at the ready to cut an old woman loose for the sake of money.

'No,' Evelyn said firmly. She placed a plate of home-made pumpkin pie in front of Izzy and sat back. 'You have enough on your plate without all of this nonsense. No one can force me to do anything.'

'My plate is looking very clean and empty at the moment,' Izzy returned.

'So you finally took my advice and picked that phone up and spoke to your brother?' Evelyn's brown eyes sparked with lively interest, her own problems temporarily set aside. 'I knew there was something you wanted to tell me. An old woman can sense these things.'

Izzy reflected that *this* was exactly why she had no intention of returning to Hawaii until she had sorted out the situation here. No, she wasn't obliged to, but where did decency and a sense of fair play go if you only did what was right because you were obliged to?

Izzy had fled Hawaii after her heart had been broken. And she had fled to the place where her mother had grown up, feeling an overpowering need somehow to *be close* to her mum in the wake of her disastrous affair with Jefferson.

The yearning just to *feel* that the spirit of her mother was close by had been silly, childish and irrational, but it had also been overwhelming enough for her to heed its insistence.

She'd rooted out the tin that was stuffed with old photos, postcards and pretty much everything she had gathered over the years before her parents had died. She had pored over faded photos of the sprawling ranch where her mother had spent her childhood before she had left home at eighteen and begun a second life in England. She had squinted at pictures of Nanny Scott, the grandparents she had only met once and all the pretty young people who had crowded her mother's teenage years. And then, heart swollen with sadness, whimsy and nostalgia, she had dumped all her responsibilities at the hotel where she had been working and quite simply *fled*.

Of course, she'd felt guilty at leaving her brother in the lurch, but she had made sure that everything was up to date, and she'd known that Nat would be able to take over temporarily. She'd also known that Max would descend and everything would be sorted because that was what he did. He wielded a rod of iron, gave commands, issued orders and *things got done*.

She'd felt far too bruised for any residual guilt about running away to anchor her in a place she no longer wanted to be, doing a job she hadn't the heart to do, however privileged she might be to have had it in the first place.

It was as if her wounded heart had made her face all those long years of living in a wilderness, learning how to manage a life without the love and input of parents, watching and envying her friends and the relationships they had with their parents.

So often her youthful heart had twisted when friends had moaned, because at least they'd had a mum and dad to moan about. Max and James had both done their best for her but there'd been only so much her brothers were capable of doing. She had stared deep into the void left by her parents' death and, in the wake of Jefferson and her bitter disillusionment, had been driven to confront it, to search for that missing *something,* which foolishly she had thought she might find if she went back to where her mother had lived.

She'd known that the big house, as her mother had called it, had long been sold, along with the vineyards. She hadn't gone there expecting to walk into her mother's childhood home. But just *being* in the area was soothing and she had been over the moon to find that Evelyn was still there when she had visited the cottage.

She'd half-expected her brother to ferret her out. He had sufficient clout to get someone to locate her within seconds, but he hadn't, and it had given her a chance to really connect with Evelyn. And, over a couple of weeks, she'd heard about the problems she was having, trying to hang onto the cottage in the face of ever-insistent demands that she sell to the guy who had bought the big house, and the even bigger house that adjoined it, so that two medium-sized vineyards could be turned into one enormous one. Another greedy developer with no scruples.

Evelyn had also been there to hear about *her* troubles and she had no intention of abandoning the older woman now, in her hour of need.

Not if she could help it.

'Well?' Evelyn pressed. 'I'm tired of thinking about my dreadful woes. Tell me some good news. And I know you've got good news! I may be old but my eyes are in perfect working condition. What did that brother of yours have to say? Gosh, my dear, I wish I had had the opportunity to meet all of you so that I could put faces to the names. I wish I knew what James and Max looked like in the flesh, and not just in those pictures you showed me on your phone.'

Izzy surfaced from her thoughts. Obligingly, she told Evelyn about her phone call, which she had been hugging to herself for the past few hours. Yes, she had spoken to Max, after a lot of procrastination. He hadn't hunted her down he had listened to Mia, thank God, and had chosen to hang back but, even so, he would only have done so reluctantly.

Izzy had been terrified when she'd made that call to tell him that there was a chance she would be staying on in California because of a muddle with Evelyn's accommodation.

She had worried that he would be fuming. Silently, aggressively, *scarily* fuming. She'd expected him to order her back and had been geared for an argument. But he'd been great. He'd told her he'd been touring the islands, much to her amazement, because she couldn't remember her brother *ever* doing *anything* that didn't involve an office, a computer and an army of yes-men lining up to do as told. And he'd assured her that everything was covered. Had told her that when she did return they would talk about what she wanted to do instead of what he wanted her to do.

Rather than ask *Who? What? Why?* and *When?*, and risk a change of heart, she had rung off and counted her blessings.

She reached for the note again and gazed at it before looking at Evelyn.

'You won't be going to have tea with that guy,' she said quietly but firmly. She reached across the table and held the older woman's hands between hers. Evelyn was as thin as a bird and Izzy could feel the bulge of her veins under her transparently pale skin. She was strong enough, and got a lot of exercise tending to her garden, but it still felt as though a puff of wind might blow her away.

'I've got to get it out of the way.' Evelyn sighed.

'No,' Izzy said. '*You* don't. *I* do.'

Gabriel Ricci looked at his watch and frowned because the woman was running late.

He had issued the invitation for five-thirty. He'd figured that that would be roughly when someone in her late seventies would probably be sitting down for a cup of tea, coffee or hot chocolate and a slice of cake, having had an afternoon nap of some sort. It was an assumption made on absolutely no concrete evidence because he hadn't actually had a cup of tea with anyone elderly at five-thirty in the afternoon in his life before.

Five-thirty was the very peak of his working day. Cups of tea and slices of cake were the last things on his mind. However, needs must. But it was still irritating to find himself waiting, because he had reached a position of such power and influence in his life that he usually never had to wait for anyone any more. He beckoned, and they duly appeared exactly when they were meant to.

How life had changed, he reflected idly. He looked around the stunning sitting room with its pale colours, lavish artwork and its view of acres upon acres of vineyards outside, rows upon rows in perfect symmetry, marching in exquisite formation towards the horizon.

He could still remember the cramped house he had grown up in—the dingy paintwork, the meagre patch of grass outside that had had to multi-function as back garden, vegetable plot and place to hang the washing on those hot summer days in Brooklyn. He and his parents had lived cheek to jowl with their neighbours, and life had been crowded and chaotic. It was a place where the toughest rose to the surface and the weakest were either to be protected or allowed to sink to the bottom.

Against this backdrop, his devoted parents had managed to nurture the importance of education and the need to get out or go under. There were many times when Gabriel had resented the repeated mantra to 'study hard and make something of yourself'. Because slacking off and having fun had been an irresistible temptation, especially when he'd known that he could have been the leader of the pack with the snap of a finger. He was big, he was street-sharp and he was fearless. But the mantra had sunk in and he had had too much love and respect for his hard-working Italian parents to walk away from their teachings.

He'd studied. He'd worked hard. He'd ended up at MIT studying engineering, and after that at Harvard, doing a PhD in business. He hadn't set his sights on climbing the ladder. Climbing wasn't going to do. He'd set his eyes on soaring to the very top of the ladder. Soaring was something he was in favour of. He wasn't going to replicate his father's life, taking orders from people dumber than him but with money, lineage and connections. He'd raced to the top of the food chain and savoured the freedom and respect that came with great wealth and even greater power.

He had politely turned away all the lucrative offers from the giants and instead, unannounced, had headed straight through the front door of a small, family-run investment company that was slowly being ground into the dust by the big boys in the business.

Sitting here now, Gabriel could still smile at the memory of that small company, with whom he still kept in close contact, because that had been his springboard and he had chosen wisely. He had catapulted them out of gridlock, got them back on the race track and had seen them steer a course through the minefield of threatening competition all around them. When they'd sold the company two years after he'd joined, they'd made millions and Gabriel had made even more.

The rest… Well, he was feared now. He had long ago said goodbye to that street-fighting Brooklyn boy who had never quite belonged because he'd been too ambitious, too smart, too focused on finding a way out. Life hadn't been easy in the years since but it had been good, at least financially—better than good.

Good enough not to sit here, at nearly six in the evening, waiting for the Scott woman to show up.

He was standing up, impatiently moving to pace the room, when the door to the sitting room was pushed open and he looked round, seeing first Marie, his housekeeper, and then immediately behind her…

Gabriel stopped dead in his tracks.

He'd been expecting a woman in her late seventies. He'd known what she looked like. He'd had a photo of her emailed to him prior to this meeting.

Instead, he was looking at a young woman, as slender as a reed with silvery white-blonde hair that tumbled in curls past her shoulders and down her back. Her skin was satin-smooth and her eyes cornflower blue—as clear as crystal.

She was dressed in dungarees and one of the straps had slipped off her shoulder, revealing a cream vest underneath and the shadowy curve of a small breast.

He was annoyed at the sudden lapse of self-control but, even as he stifled it, he could still feel the stirring of his libido and the uninvited, utterly misplaced notion that this sort of immediate, knee-jerk physical reaction was just not him—and *that* annoyed him even more.

He abruptly broke the silence while moving forward.

'And you are?'

His voice was cool and soft, and feathered down Izzy's spine like the promise of danger.

What had she been expecting? Not this.

The house she had approached only distantly resembled the much smaller place her grandparents had owned, the one captured in that handful of faded photographs Izzy had lovingly stashed. It had clearly been extended over the years and was now the fitting palace of a billionaire, although she wasn't quite certain how long the guy had owned it. According to Evelyn, it had been bought and sold twice and, she had confided the evening before, he was the last buyer and recently on the scene. He'd done all the renovations, though, and Evelyn knew that because she had seen those very renovations in progress over the better part of a year, during which time the vineyards continued to be maintained to the very highest standard.

Yet she had still been impressed by the scale of the place. It was vast. A vast white mansion fronted by a courtyard that could have housed a hundred cars with room to spare.

She'd stared but was undaunted. She was familiar

with staggering wealth. She knew what it could and couldn't buy, and a seventy-nine-year-old woman was not one of those things on the table for sale, and she intended to make that very clear.

She'd been shown in by a young girl with a cheerful demeanour and not many words, and she'd been feeling pleasantly bolshie until now. Until she stood in this exquisite sitting room, with the door quietly shutting behind her, staring at the most beautiful man she had ever seen in her life.

He was tall, a few inches over six feet, with a body that was lean and muscular, as sinewy as an athlete's. He was wearing a short-sleeved white polo shirt and dark trousers that rode just low enough on his lean hips to emphasise the taut narrowing of his waist and the length of his legs. His dark hair was slightly too long, curling against the collar of his polo shirt, and he had lashes to die for, lush and dark, shielding eyes that were as cool as black ice. And he was burnished bronze, exotically stunning.

He took her breath away and the confidence with which she had sauntered into the house evaporated as fast as dew on a summer's morning.

'Well?'

Izzy discovered that her mouth was dry and she averted her eyes because the temptation to stare was overwhelming. Unfortunately, eyes averted, she could still see the image of him in her head, so drop-dead gorgeous with olive skin, eyes as dark as midnight and features that were so perfectly chiselled that for a second you could almost overlook the glacial lack of welcome in his expression.

Not for long, though, as his coldly delivered question snapped her right back down to earth with a bump.

'Izzy Stowe,' she said abruptly. He strolled towards her and she backed away a couple of inches and folded her arms in a gesture that was semi-belligerent, semi-defensive.

'And you are standing in my living room because…?'

'You sent a note to Evelyn Scott. You wanted to discuss the business of bullying her into selling the cottage.' Defiant words, she thought, which was precisely the opposite of how she was feeling. Intimidated, was more like it. She shuddered to think how Evelyn would have coped. Evelyn was lively, but she was older, and might have been easily cowed by this kind of man. Frankly, who wouldn't? He looked the sort who'd had dungeons constructed for anyone who dared get in his way.

'I have no desire to talk to anyone but Mrs Scott. The door is behind you, Miss Stowe.'

With great effort, Izzy stayed her ground.

How rude! But why should she be surprised? Anyone who was happy to use bully-boy tactics on an old woman wasn't exactly going to be the sort who prioritised good manners and common courtesy, was he?

'Evelyn has given me full permission to deal with

this situation.' She remained where she was but she badly wanted to turn tail and flee.

'Your qualifications being…?'

'We're old friends and I want to look out for her.'

'Isn't she capable of looking out for herself? She seemed very determined in her replies to my legal team when they've been in contact with her.'

'Would you mind if I sit?' Izzy noted his hesitation and knew that he was weighing up his options. He was a busy man, she guessed, with limited time to spare running round for an elusive old woman. Another day waiting for a meeting would be an unnecessary delay and maybe he was weighing up the odds of the result being exactly the same—no Evelyn but *her* again.

He nodded curtly to one of the chairs and Izzy tentatively inched towards it and sat. Immediately she felt at a disadvantage, because he continued to tower over her, but her legs had been wobbly.

'Speak.'

One word delivered as he continued to stand over her, staring down through narrowed eyes.

Izzy noted that the invitation to take tea had obviously been rescinded now that she had been the one to show up rather than Evelyn. He hadn't even offered her a glass of water and he showed zero signs of remedying the oversight.

'Would you mind sitting?' she asked. 'I don't want to have this conversation craning my neck.'

She half-expected him to ignore her but instead

he dragged a footstool over and positioned it directly in front of her so that she had no option but to look at him. Up close like this, he was even more forbidding, because he was so much closer—close enough for her to breathe in the warm, woody scent of whatever aftershave he was wearing, and definitely close enough to see the unforgiving coldness in his dark eyes.

'Evelyn has confided in me about her situation.' Izzy kept her voice even and calm. His eyes were sooty-black and scarily watchful, and she could sense her every word being carefully dissected and meticulously inspected from every angle. She shivered.

'Are you related to Mrs Scott?'

'*Miss* Scott. Evelyn never married.'

'That's of little relevance to this situation.'

'Is it, Mr Ricci?' Izzy asked quietly. 'That cottage is where Evelyn's lived most of her adult life. Well over five decades. It's all she's ever known. She has no husband, no partner and no children. Do you really think she's going to jump for joy at the thought of leaving the one place in the world that represents stability for her? Furthermore, she has all her friends within driving distance, and all her social meetings happen in the town. Yet you want to drive her away from the one place she's ever called home.'

'That's a very rousing speech, Miss Stowe, but I don't care for the emotive vocabulary. I have not been using bullying tactics and my desire is not to *drive* anyone anywhere. Nor, for that matter, is it any of my concern whether the woman never chose to get married.'

'You want to buy her cottage!'

'At a price that's way over the market odds.'

'There's no price high enough to dislodge someone from the only place they know as home.'

'I beg to differ.'

Without warning, he vaulted upright, and Izzy followed his unhurried progress to a buzzer on the wall. Within seconds, the very same young lady who had shown her to the sitting room was knocking on the door.

'Something to drink, Miss Stowe? Before I persuade you that it would be in Miss Scott's best interests to take the offer I'm making and run with it.'

The sheer arrogance of the man was mind-blowing, Izzy thought. He was prepared to hear her out but it was clear that his mind was already made up. As Evelyn had pointed out, though, no one could force her hand. He'd probably figured he'd be onto a winner by confronting Evelyn face to face, oozing menace, muttering veiled threats and then just waiting for her to crumble in fear.

Gabriel Ricci, Izzy concluded, was everything she disliked in a person. He was rude, ruthless, arrogant and utterly incapable of seeing anyone's agenda but his own.

She was guiltily aware that in many respects he

reminded her of Max, although her brother had very logical reasons for being the way he was.

When she'd been much younger—too young after the death of their parents really to understand the complexities of the situation—she had absolutely *hated* her older brother for his inflexible, disciplinarian approach. He had overseen everything she'd done with a baleful and unforgiving eye, forcing her to toe the line, refusing her all the little liberties her friends had enjoyed. Permission had had to be granted for the smallest of excursions and, as she had become a teenager, he had become stricter yet.

Only when James had sat her down one afternoon, and gently tried to explain why Max felt driven to protect her, had she come close to understanding those heavy-handed tactics. He had taken over as the head of the household and it had fallen to him to make sure as little changed as humanly possible for both James and her. It had fallen to him to run the company until James had been able to step up to the plate and help, which he had. So he had ruled with a rod of steel, and it was only recently that she wondered what had been lost for him in the process.

But what was *this* man's excuse for being a complete bastard?

He clearly wasn't in the business of trying to buy the cottage because he cared about the fate of the occupant. This was the first time he had even deigned to make personal contact with Evelyn. Prior to that,

he had handed the messy business to one of his un-
derlings to sort out.

'I'll have a glass of water,' she said coolly and he
shrugged and turned to the young girl.

'A glass of water,' he said. 'Snd a bottle of Cabernet Sauvignon—with two glasses.'

'I won't be drinking any wine,' Izzy informed
him abruptly. 'I'm not here to have drinks, Mr Ricci.
I'm here to tell you that Evelyn won't be selling the
cottage and, if you don't stop pestering her, I'll have
no option but to get in touch with a lawyer.'

'This particular Cabernet is extremely good.
Powerful yet elegant, and one hundred percent sus-
tainable.'

'Have you heard a word I've just said?' She fell
into temporary seething silence until the housekeeper returned with drinks as requested, carefully
pouring Gabriel a glass and handing Izzy the water
she had asked for.

She could barely contain her anger at his indif-
ference to what she had to say.

'Well?' she snapped, as he took his time appreciating the wine.

'This is my first foray into the wine business,'
he informed her, swirling his glass and then taking
a sip as he coolly looked at her over the rim of the
glass. He sauntered to the window and gazed out for
a few seconds before turning to look at her.

Izzy said nothing, skewered into silence. Buried
under her fury and feeling of impotence was the re-

luctant recognition that there was something mes-
merising about the man. Her mouth wanted to hang
open and she desperately had to make an effort to
cling to her self-control because she knew with un-
erring gut instinct, if he sensed *any* weakness, he
would take advantage of it with the ruthless speed
of a born predator.

'I like this part of the valley and I like the size
of the vineyards. Combined with the neighbouring estate, I have extremely promising acreage.' He
paused to have another mouthful of wine and then
he strolled back to where he had been sitting. This
time, he leaned towards her, filling the space between them with such suffocating force that Izzy
automatically slightly leaned back. A glass of water
gave absolutely no Dutch courage.

'Here's the thing,' he said softly. 'Your friend is
sitting on a patch of land that is in the midst of my
vineyards. It is an oasis, I am sure, at this very point
in time. However, should Miss Scott fail to sell, I
have every intention of buying the land that abuts
her oasis. I intend to keep this house for myself, my
personal estate whether I am occupying it or not, but
I will require suitable accommodation for the man
who will effectively be running the show, and his
staff. It will be a business of no small scale.

'There will, first of all, be the chaos of a compound being built. Your friend, I fear, will find herself surrounded by the bustle of people coming and
going. It will no longer be quite the oasis it currently

is. In due course, I intend to extend further and have a boutique hotel on the grounds for a handful of wine connoisseurs who want to sample the workings of the vineyard first-hand, taste the wines, watch the process from grape to barrel.' He shrugged elegantly. 'This, I fear, is the way of the world. Nothing ever stays the same.'

Izzy gaped, fascinated despite herself at the picture being painted before her dismayed eyes. Every word he said left her in no doubt that life as Evelyn knew it would change immeasurably. Perhaps not with the purchase of the vineyards, although all that increased production would surely ramp up activity, but should he buy the land around her then she would no longer have any peace.

'I have offered Miss Scott a remarkable deal,' Gabriel continued, while Izzy mentally grappled with how *a remarkable deal* could incorporate ruining someone's life. 'I will personally see to it that she has whatever other house she desires in Napa. Her friends are here? She could be closer to them. Furthermore, I will ensure that whatever house she wants is done to the standard she requires, and has as much or as little land as she deems necessary so that she can continue to fulfil her gardening exploits to her heart's content.'

'But it won't be her *home*,' Izzy whispered, fighting off the temptation to be lulled into giving his offer house room despite herself.

'A home is a moveable feast, Miss Stowe. Should she turn down my offer, I will not pursue the matter, but she could very well find that selling the property at a later date, on the open market, might not get her a quarter of what she would get right now from me. Who would want to buy a dated cottage surrounded by someone else's land and subject to all the disagreeable bustle that a full-scale business might entail? I certainly wouldn't, should she contemplate selling to me at a later date when disillusionment has had time to set in.'

He sat back and tilted his head to one side. 'I should stress that this is a one-time opportunity, Miss Stowe. Convey that message to her. I intend to be here for another fortnight but I will want your friend's decision by the end of the week. I will begin talks with Ferguson about buying his land at that point and, once that's been set in motion, this offer will no longer be available.'

This was her cue to leave. She could read it in his expression. He'd allowed her to have her little moment but he'd known that his powerful argument would throw her, as it had.

'I'm not scared of your threats, Mr Ricci.' She rose to her feet to find that her legs still felt wobbly.

'I seldom threaten. I find it's a tactic that pays few dividends.'

Izzy stared at him. He was so ridiculously beautiful, and yet he chilled her to the bone, because there was nothing there that was warm or even *human*.

The tense silence was broken by the sound of racing feet, and then the door to the sitting room was flung open and there, standing in the doorway, was a child.

CHAPTER TWO

'ROSA!'

Gabriel registered his daughter's breathless presence in the doorway at roughly the same time as he clocked the astonished expression on Izzy's face. Both were a source of annoyance, in varying degrees and for different reasons.

His daughter, because she should be getting ready to wind down and go to bed.

What the hell was that dragon of her nanny doing? She was paid handsomely to make sure that his daughter's routine went unchanged, even though Rosa wasn't at her mother's house in New York. She wouldn't be slacking off. She might not be top of his Christmas card list but she was completely trustworthy when it came to his daughter...so what the heck was this all about?

And Izzy, because her presence under his roof had nothing to do with the personal side of his life. She was there to nit-pick over the business with the cottage, and in Gabriel's world business was never allowed to push past any unopened doors. Rosa was his six-year-old daughter and he didn't need the woman's curiosity clouding the issue of why she was sitting in his living room.

And curious she was. Her aquamarine eyes were ablaze with curiosity and surprise.

'What are you doing down here?' Gabriel covered ground fast and now scooped up his daughter, who wrapped her legs around his waist while peering animatedly over his shoulder to where Izzy continued to stare with undisguised interest.

'Who's she?' Rosa piped up by way of reply.

Gabriel frowned because he wasn't inclined to get into a conversation about Izzy.

'*She*...is about to leave,' he said, heaving his daughter back to the ground and holding out his hand for her to take, which she did, while craning back to inspect Izzy. 'And where is Bella?'

It never failed to amaze him that a name that translated as 'beautiful' could apply to someone as ferociously unappealing as his daughter's nanny.

Bella Esposito was in her mid-sixties and had been Rosa's nanny for the past three years. A retired deputy head at an all girls' school in downtown Manhattan, she had been brought on board by his ex-wife Bianca, and had approached the position with the zeal of a despot accustomed to being obeyed.

'She is the only one I would consider for the job,' Bianca had announced, at the time having dismissed the previous nanny with five minutes' notice because she had failed to take the job as seriously as she should have. 'She's related and I trust her completely. Young girls do not have the required approach to discipline that Rosa needs!'

Bella was a cousin of a cousin of an aunt and, when it came to discipline, she had a first-class degree in instilling it.

There were strict rules to cover all occasions. Orders were barked, bedtimes were obeyed to the very second, snacks were banned and leisure activities were supervised with rigour.

Gabriel privately loathed the woman but what could he do? Aside from the fact that he worked so, as now, the time Rosa spent with him required the presence of a nanny, he was also in the position of having his hands tied.

Bianca would have enjoyed nothing better than making life difficult for him. Quibble over the nanny, and she would conspire to withhold his daughter from him, whatever the distribution of custody. As it stood, she was prone to changing dates with next to no notice and threatening to return to court for full custody if he complained. Would she? It was a risk he had no intention of taking, and neither was he prepared to antagonise his ex to the point where the axe of retaliation might fall upon his daughter's unsuspecting head.

He had bitten down the urge to wield his influence so many times that he had lost count.

Right now, Rosa was with him for three weeks of

her summer holiday, and on the horizon lay a fight that he could only contemplate with growing horror. Bianca, she had informed him only a fortnight ago, was intent on returning to Italy. Her mother needed her, she had piously declared, which was nothing short of a joke, considering she and her mother were as close as two combatants in a boxing ring.

Was she angling for yet more money? Or was she being serious? She didn't stand a chance in hell of removing his daughter from his orbit, surely, but he wasn't willing to take any chances. He would have to hang back, however much it enraged him, and use persuasion to woo her away from the idea of leaving New York.

Truthfully, he worked long hours and led a lifestyle that was not ideally suited to parenting a six-year-old child, even though all that work was fuelled by his driving need to make sure that his daughter got the very best. Every hour he worked was to give her everything he possibly could.

He did his utmost when Rosa was with him but sometimes deals could not be ignored and his ex-wife knew that all too well. As she knew about his love life. Who didn't? He had been snapped on more than one occasion with some passing beauty on his arm gazing up adoringly, little knowing that she would soon join her predecessors as footnotes in his love life.

And on top of that...

Gabriel was at the very pinnacle of the pecking

order. In the world of business, he ruled the roost, with fingers in many pies. He was the darling of the *Financial Times* and a past pin-up on magazines, from business to gossip.

He had got to that position by dint of sacrifice but he was very well aware that deep down, buried under the self-assurance that was so much a part and parcel of his powerful personality, lay uneasy guilt.

He'd been married at twenty-six and divorced by thirty. Bianca had been descended from Italian royalty, and a far cry from people of his own background, which had been rooted in poverty. She had been flamboyant, beautiful, and demanding of attention. But he had put work first. Where she had wanted parties and social events and opportunities to parade her voluptuous beauty, he had given her diamonds and pearls and turned his back on her needs. He had done what he had always done best and focused on his empire, leaving her to drift into the arms of another man.

Who could blame her? was the thought that sometimes kept him awake in the early hours of the morning. The tough Brooklyn kid who had seen work as his passport to freedom had proved more resilient than the wealthy, urbane empire builder she had fallen for and signed up to.

Worse was the realisation that he had been *relieved* that the marriage had crashed and burned, and the realisation that he had found her intensely annoying almost from day one.

But he refused to allow his daughter to become
a casualty of the divorce, so he played by the rules
set out for him, driven by guilt and uncertain how
far he could push his luck, given his lifestyle, which
would never change.

It was a mess.

Even more of a mess now.

He surfaced to hear his daughter whispering that
Nanny Bella wasn't feeling very well.

Gabriel stilled. He half-turned and shot a sideways look at Izzy, who appeared to be consumed
with interest in a business magazine that had been
lying on the walnut table in front of the sofa, studi-
ously ignoring the drama being played out, despite
her initial curiosity.

'Ill?' Was there a germ on this planet equipped to
get past the woman's suit of armour? he wondered.

Yet, illness or not, where the hell was she? This
was the first time Rosa had ever ventured out of her
bedroom while Bella was on officious duty.

He hesitated, torn between releasing his iron control over his private life and asking Izzy to keep an
eye on Rosa and carrying his impressionable daughter up with him to find out what was going on.

'Would you mind…?' He led Rosa across the
room and paused as Izzy looked up at him. 'My
daughter…' he said heavily, raking his fingers
through his dark hair and briefly glancing away.
'Some situation with her nanny…'

'I'm Rosa,' Rosa helpfully piped up, stretching out her hand. 'Who are you?'

'I'm Izzy.'

'I love your hair.'

Izzy smiled and met Gabriel's midnight-black eyes. 'It's fine. I'll stay here with your daughter if you want to go and see what's happened to the nanny.'

He didn't want to do that. Izzy could see reluctance stamped all over his lean, dark face. He hadn't expected his daughter to barge in just when he'd been about to send her on her way, and he certainly hadn't expected to end up having to leave her in the room while he went to find out what was going on with the errant nanny in his employ.

He'd been put in an unenviable position. Izzy suspected that he was the sort of guy who was in love with self-control, so being put in unenviable positions would be very low down the list of things he appreciated.

She couldn't help but feel an uncharitable twinge of satisfaction that he had been temporarily waylaid.

It had taken every ounce of willpower to try and bury herself in the boring business magazine lying on the table in front of her. She had picked it up because her innate politeness had forbidden her from ogling the beautiful child who had entered the room with too much overt curiosity, or marvelling that a man who was made of ice could actually be a dad, and a very affectionate and loving one from the looks of it.

The cardboard cut-out, one-dimensional picture she had had in her head no longer seemed quite so straightforward.

'What are you doing here?'

Izzy grinned, liking Rosa's precociousness. She was a stunning child, with long, dark hair tucked behind her ears, an olive complexion and huge, dark eyes. She was in her pyjamas, which involved a lot of coloured dinosaurs clamouring over highly patterned terrain. Izzy approved. In her hand were a few sheets of paper.

'What have you got here?' Izzy asked, with interest.

'Drawings. For Dad.' She held them out and Izzy spent a few minutes admiring the art work and making the right appreciative noises while with one ear she listened out for returning footsteps on the wooden floor.

'Are you here for the weekend?' She smiled and reached for the crayon in Rosa's hand without thinking.

'Three weeks. Mom's gone to the house in Tuscany and Dad's got me while she's away.' She shrugged. 'It's his turn. I prefer being with dad anyway, even if he's at work a lot.'

'And Bella is the girl who looks after you?'

None of my business, Izzy was thinking as her hand skimmed absently on the blank space on the paper, doodling one of the dinosaurs on Rosa's pyjamas, giving it expression, movement and an outfit. *I'm here to do a job, to sort out Evelyn. This man is unscrupulous and the last thing I need is to get involved in his family dynamic...*

'Bella isn't *a girl*,' Rosa said scornfully. 'She's a witch and I hate her. Wow. I love that drawing! Can you do another?' Just like that she had switched from loathing for the nanny to excitable admiration at what Izzy had done. But Izzy had no time to reply because the door was pushed open and this time standing in the doorway, just as Rosa had stood in the doorway a short while ago, was Gabriel, devoid of the cool composure she had seen in him before.

'Bella's collapsed,' he said abruptly. He looked at Rosa. 'I could call an ambulance out, but by the time it got here it would probably be faster for me to drive her to the hospital.'

'What's wrong?' Izzy leapt to her feet in consternation.

'My guess would be appendicitis, judging from what she's managed to say…and possibly a ruptured one. I have to go. Rosa…' He raked frustrated fingers through his dark hair, his body restless with tension and urgency. 'A hospital is not a suitable place. I will have to talk to doctors…'

'I can come.' The offer was out there before Izzy could think about it. She saw the struggle on his face, but time was of the essence, and he nodded.

'It would help. I will be down in a few minutes.

If you wouldn't mind meeting me with Rosa by the front door…we need to move at speed.'

Izzy did as she was told, barely thinking as she hurried to the front door with Rosa, grabbing the crayons and paper and stuffing them into her bag, because she would have to occupy the child while her father did what he needed to do.

He could have left Rosa behind with her, but of course why would he? He didn't know her from Adam.

How ironic that Izzy had come out here to try and imbibe the spirit of her mother, find solace in her memory in the wake of her broken heart, yet in the very house in which Beverley Stowe had grown up she felt nothing but Gabriel's overwhelming personality. Now here she was, swept along on a wave of unexpected circumstances, and whimsy could not have been further from her mind. She could have dug her heels in and left him to his own devices, to sort out an ill nanny with his daughter in tow, but that option had not even occurred to Izzy.

She was barely aware of the drive to hospital. Rosa clung to her in the back seat of the black four-by-four, scared and silenced by the tension. In the front, Bella moaned while Gabriel drove fast, his body language signalling complete focus on what was going on. As soon as they made it to hospital, he turned to Izzy and, in between giving orders for a wheelchair to be brought for Bella, said that he would meet her as soon as he could in the reception area. He hugged Rosa, stooping to murmur a few reassuring words, and disentangled her even as he glanced up to where Izzy was staring down at them.

'Thank you,' he said gruffly.

Then he vanished behind the rush of people sweeping Bella away.

Izzy had never babysat anyone before in her life. Her dealings with young kids had largely been confined to meeting some of her friend Mia's nephews and nieces now and again. Now, though, something fired up inside her as she held the little girl's hand and hunted down the reception area, which was half-empty.

She felt a rush of emotion because she could *feel* Rosa's confusion. Being deprived of her dad frightened her, even for this short space of time, and Izzy could understand that fear. Heck, hadn't she spent so much of her life experiencing something very like it?

She chatted all the while until she felt Rosa relax, her voice calm and soothing. She spent the next hour or so entertaining her by drawing whatever she wanted until, at a little after nine, Rosa fell asleep without warning and with the innocence of a child, her head resting on Izzy's shoulder, her small body softening into slumber.

Izzy breathed in Rosa's child smell, rested her head on hers and thought about her own childhood, but not in a way that was maudlin or self-pitying. She thought of her loneliness after her parents had died and the way she had hugged it to herself because there'd been only so much her brothers could do to alleviate it. She thought of Jefferson and wondered whether she'd been so desperate to *love* and to *be loved* that she had overlooked all the signs of a person who had never been right for her.

She mused about this quest of hers in Napa Valley, hoping for memories to be the balm that might heal her heart. She knew, in an accepting rush, that the only person who could help her deal with her broken heart was herself. Unlike Rosa, she wasn't a child any longer.

It was after ten and she had drifted off to sleep by the time Gabriel returned, gently nudging her back to consciousness.

Izzy blinked, stifled a yawn and eased Rosa off her so that she could straighten.

He looked exhausted and, for the first time since she had met him, practically human.

'Have you…? Is everything okay?'

'Thank you for staying here with Rosa. I appreciate it.' He lifted Rosa, who remained asleep, and nestled her against him, waiting for Izzy so that they could leave, briefly explaining what had happened as they walked towards his car, which mysteriously was waiting for them. He must have ordered someone to bring it to the front of the building.

'I should be heading back.' Izzy hesitated and glanced over at him. The breath caught in her throat. He was so extravagantly beautiful, she thought distractedly, especially right now with Rosa curled into him. She had managed a brief, whispered chat to Evelyn while Rosa had been asleep against her, and had detected the anxiety in her voice when she had asked how the meeting had gone. Izzy hadn't had the heart to tell her that it hadn't quite gone according to plan. The man who wanted to buy her out had no intention of being Mr Nice Guy, whatever the circumstances.

It was easy to start feeling gooey and soppy, because there was something so touching about a dad and his kid, but that was irrelevant. Just because a sudden emergency had blown his cool for a couple of hours didn't mean that he had suddenly had a personality transplant.

'You haven't eaten.'

'I'm fine.' She blushed and looked away but he was already opening the door for her, having settled Rosa in the back seat.

'How has Rosa been?'

Izzy hesitated and then dropped into the passenger seat, waiting until the car roared into life before talking.

He wanted to find out about his daughter and that was only to be expected. He would want to know whether she'd been upset or in any way traumatised by the sudden tempest that had blown up.

They maintained a truce for the duration of the drive back to his mansion as Izzy told him what she and Rosa had done whilst they'd waited for him to sort out the situation. And, once inside, the thought of digging her heels in and refusing the food on offer seemed a huge effort. She was tired, she was hungry and anyway, having done him this favour, maybe he would be more amenable to listening and really taking on board what she had to say about Evelyn.

She wasn't *socialising* with the man, nor was she going to be swayed because she'd glimpsed a side to him that wasn't entirely objectionable. It made sense to be here, she thought, having been left in the kitchen while he disappeared to settle Rosa, because their conversation wasn't over and this might just be the perfect time to reintroduce it. She perked up just thinking about it.

She waited at the kitchen table and stiffened, immediately nervous, as he breezed back in and began fumbling through the fridge and in cupboards, extracting items of food at random. Bread, cheese, tomatoes and various other items wrapped in deli containers were piled onto the counter.

Did he even know the layout of his own kitchen? Izzy wondered as he continued to open and shut drawers, finally locating cutlery and a couple of wine glasses.

'No, thank you.' She covered the glass with her hand. 'I really can't hang around.'

Gabriel shrugged and began slicing the bread into uneven wedges.

'Join me, or are you in too much of a rush to escape even though you're hungry?'

'I only came here because you wanted to know how Rosa was, Mr Ricci, and it was only fair that I reassured you that she was fine. I haven't changed my stance about you and about trying to convince you that what you're doing to Evelyn is a terrible idea.'

'You've met my daughter. I think it's appropriate that we drop the formal address. My name is Gabriel. So feel free to call me Gabriel and I'll call you Izzy. Rosa likes you. She woke up just long enough to tell me that as I was settling her.'

Izzy bristled because she was sitting here, intent on not relaxing into chit chat, but he was tucking into the food without restraint and taking the conversation away from the cottage.

She wasn't going to let him think that he had wrapped it all up in a five-minute warning talk, and that once she'd gone he'd be able to wash his hands of her.

'She's very engaging.'

'I'm not sure Bella would agree with you,' Gabriel said wryly. 'But, in fairness, she hasn't made life particularly easy for her nanny. Drop the pride and eat some of this food, Izzy. It's not much but you must be starving.'

'I'm good, thank you, Mr… *Gabriel*. I just don't want you to think that everything's forgotten, that the business with the nanny has overtaken the reason I came here to see you in the first place. I don't want you to imagine that you can threaten me into retreat.'

'Pick your battles,' he returned softly, glancing at her. 'You're not going to win this one.' He nodded at the food and she ignored him. Her taxi would arrive soon enough—she had taken a couple of seconds to order one—but where did they go from here?

'Would you at least come to the cottage?' she ventured, because if she left without any follow up in place she felt the next correspondence, should Evelyn fail to accept his offer, would be something informing her that he had begun the process of buying the rest of the acreage around the cottage and to expect the builders soon.

'Why would I do that?'

Their eyes met, bright blue colliding with darkest black, and again she felt a shiver of awareness, a hint of danger that went beyond anything to do with the cottage and the silken threats of what he could do. It was a hint of danger that confused and panicked her. She was too *aware* of him. When his eyes rested on her, she felt a lot more than just angry. She felt… *unsettled*, as though a part of her *enjoyed* whatever weird, incomprehensible sensations he managed to stir deep inside.

He unsettled her on a physical level, and she hated that, because it was distracting and bewildering. Jefferson had left her disillusioned with her first foray into the business of a relationship. She'd been badly let down. She'd fled, disappointed and embittered by her experience, so why was she finding her eyes drawn to this man?

'Perhaps if you met Evelyn…'

'I would have…' he relaxed back to look at her coolly '…had you not decided to jump to her rescue and represent her in her absence. What is your relationship with her, anyway? I don't believe you said.'

'I believe I did,' Izzy returned. 'Friend.' Should she tell him about her connection to the house? What would be the point? It was hardly as though the house had awakened anything inside her at all. Aside from knowing that her mother had been brought up there, it could just have been any mansion. Too much had changed from those wistful photos her mother had taken all those years ago.

While the cottage—and Evelyn—had both stirred feelings inside her, taking her back to the past and helping her recall her mother. Was that why she felt so strongly about protecting it? About not seeing it turned into something for someone else, expanded into a compound to house strangers, which would probably involve it being razed to the ground and replaced with something cold, anodyne and functional?

'You're here on holiday…' He inclined his head and his expression was both lazy and shrewdly calculating at the same time. 'And a long way from home, judging from your accent. Did you just decide to pay Miss Scott a visit out of the blue—since you insist on talking about this?'

She took a deep breath. 'Why all the questions? It doesn't matter why I'm here, does it?' She paused.

'I'd really appreciate it if you did come to the cottage and did meet Evelyn,' she said quietly. 'It might make you change your mind.'

Gabriel's eyebrows shot up. 'I assure you, Izzy, that I'm not a man who ever changes direction.'

'That's not something to brag about,' Izzy muttered.

She had spent so much of her life doing what Max told her to do: working hard to get good grades at school, studying for a degree she had minimal interest in because it made sense and would establish a clear career path, avoiding all the complications of fun relationships with boys because it had been important not to be distracted. She had finally taken a stand in throwing out Max's ideas for the hotel and imposing her own. She had found her voice, taken a deep breath and decided to use it.

So what if her stand had been a bit shaky? She had kept her plans for the hotel under wraps, trying to work out how she could break it to her brother that she didn't agree with his vision when she should have just *told* him.

Then, riding a wave of independence, she had flung herself into an ill-fated love affair, only to take the coward's way out when it had crashed and burned and disappear in search of something she now knew she would never find because her mother was in her heart and not in a pile of bricks and mortar...

But it had still been a stand. She had still dug

her heels in with Max instead of dutifully settling into the career he had carved out for her...and he respected her for it! Wonder of wonders, he'd actually said so when they'd talked at last, on the phone. And she had still broken through the ever-increasing burden of her lack of love-life and so what if she'd made a mistake?

Both events had given her a huge morale boost and the courage now not to flinch in the face of a man who was clearly accustomed to getting his own way.

'Come again?'

'I said...' Izzy looked at him with challenging eyes '...that it's not cool to be inflexible.'

Gabriel was incredulous.

He was exhausted. It had been a long evening. He had used all the authority at his disposal to ensure the very top consultant was involved in making sure Bella got the best possible medical attention. As he'd thought, it was a ruptured appendix, and her recovery would be at least a week, possibly more.

He had phoned Bianca to explain the situation and discovered, to his surprise, that she had taken herself off to the Tuscan villa that had been part of her divorce package, revitalising his uneasy suspicions that threats about her absconding to Italy with his daughter hovered on the horizon as a dangerous possibility. He hadn't been able to picture the Italian beauty suddenly turning into Florence Nightingale to care for a mother she had never had time for, but Donata Mancini lived in the Tuscan hills, so why else would his ex be there now?

Unsurprisingly, he had had to deal with Bianca's evident pleasure that he had found himself without a nanny. She had only just stopped short of crowing that he could now see for himself what full-time parenting looked like. Not that she had a clue herself, he'd been tempted to say, bearing in mind her life of pampered luxury in which, if his daughter was to be believed, bonding times with Rosa involved joint manicures at her beauty salon—an experience Rosa described with horror.

Bianca had mournfully told him about her mother's failing health and how much she was needed in Tuscany but, she had hinted nastily, perhaps it would stand in his favour if he actually proved that he could manage single-handedly with Rosa and put some of his precious work to one side *for a change*.

The last thing he needed was this conversation with Izzy. The fact that he couldn't look at the stubborn little blonde sitting in front of him without his body hiving off at a tangent was a sensation he found intensely irritating, a distraction he could do without.

It was infuriating enough that one very important area of his life could not be controlled, that no amount of power, money or influence could bring about the conclusion he wanted when it came to his daughter. He really didn't need for any more areas of his life to go off-piste.

And yet…

There was something about the blonde that made him stop dead in his tracks, even though she was the most argumentative and irritating woman he had ever met.

'You really think that insulting me is going to encourage me to meet you halfway on this?' Gabriel drawled. He shoved the plate to one side, pushed his chair away from the table and angled his long body so that he could stretch his legs out.

Each small, economical movement made for compulsive viewing.

'I wasn't insulting you, but I think it's a good thing if someone can see all points of view and… er…give other people a chance to speak their mind and make a case for what they want. I mean…' she looked around her at the impressive paintings hanging on the walls, the pale, expensive furniture and the faded, silken elegance of the Persian rug on the wooden floor '… I *know* you probably don't want to be having this conversation but do you *really* need to add to your wealth?'

There was genuine curiosity in her question because, although she had had a comfortable lifestyle, thanks to her brothers and her privileged background, she had never really understood other people's fixation with money. In fact, if anything, money had brought its own problems. Because how could you ever tell whether the people who pursued you wanted you for your money or for who you were?

Her assumption was that Gabriel came from money. He carried himself like someone born into great wealth. He had that mantle of self-confidence, that assumption of obedience that spoke of an elevated background.

For Izzy, it was a turn-off.

Gabriel said with amazement, 'Are you preaching to me about my life choices? And, yes, I really would rather *not* be having this conversation.'

Izzy decided to ignore that particular segment of what he had said. 'I suppose when you've been born into a rich background it's really tough to try and see how people feel and think who come from the opposite side of the tracks...' She pensively looked off into the distance, then frowned at her mobile phone, because the taxi was taking longer than she'd expected.

'You are an extremely challenging woman.' Gabriel gritted his teeth.

Izzy half-opened her mouth to tell him that *he* was equally challenging, and then blushed a bright red, because from the expression on his face he seemed to know exactly what was going through her head.

Her phone buzzed. The taxi had finally arrived and she leapt to her feet, relieved to be going. She would have to think about how best to make her case one more time because the man was intransigent.

Her high hopes were currently at rock bottom. If he couldn't be persuaded into seeing what the consequences of his actions would involve for Evelyn with his own eyes, then she would simply have to help the older woman adjust to a lifestyle she hadn't banked on at her age.

She was very much aware of him walking her to the front door. He emanated a powerful masculine pull that made the hairs on the back of her neck stand on end and gave her goose bumps. He was good-looking, she thought, but that wasn't it. She wasn't that shallow. Jefferson had been good-looking, in a different type of way. Blond hair and green eyes. Surfer looks. But he had been funny and free-spirited, and that was what she had been attracted to in him.

This man gave her goose bumps because of that aura of threat he wore. He would give anyone goose bumps. A charging army would stop dead in their tracks. The fact that he was drop-dead gorgeous was just a peripheral distraction.

'How long are you planning to stay in the area?'

The deep timbre of his voice interrupted the feverish train of her thoughts and she slid a sideways glance at him from under her lashes.

'I'd planned on staying…seeing this through… helping Evelyn…'

'Don't you have a job to get back to? Family? A significant other?'

'I…' She glared at him. He made her life sound bare and empty, standing there leaning against the door, watching her with lazy interest. She was only twenty-two, yet she knew that she had few friends, definitely no significant other and that there had never been any significant other until Jefferson, not even an adolescent first love. She'd launched herself into a relationship with Jefferson, high on a sense of freedom, in love with the idea of being in love— and here she was, still a virgin, because nothing had worked out. She wondered, somewhere deep down, whether anything ever would. Who knew? What she *did* know was that Jefferson had put doubts in her head that had not been there before. 'My taxi's here,' she said coolly.

'It'll wait.'

'Really?'

'Really. No one would dare pull up to this house and leave without my permission. I'm guessing that your flexibility on the lifestyle front answers my question.' He pushed himself away from the door and looked down at her for a few seconds. 'You want me to have the face-to-face conversation I had in-tended to have with your friend?'

Izzy shot him a hopeful glance and immediately felt a little unsteady on her feet. His lazy, veiled stare pinned her to the spot and sucked the breath out of her.

'You know I do.' She was aiming for cool, composed and a little sarcastic. Instead, she sounded breathless and flustered.

'Tomorrow. I'll come across to the cottage.'

'You know how to get there?'

'I have a lot of land, but I think I can work out the route to the gingerbread house without a trail of breadcrumbs guiding me.'

'There's no need to be sarcastic,' Izzy muttered. She tore her eyes away and looked down at her feet. When she next looked up, it was to find him staring at her in a way which made her feel giddy. 'What time can Evelyn expect you to come?'

'Both of you,' Gabriel told her smoothly. 'I want you there as well—not that I'm sure I have to say that, considering you've volunteered for guardian angel duty.' He opened the door for her, letting in a waft of warm, evening breeze. 'I'll be over at six.'

Izzy backed out of the door and nodded. Tomorrow. Six. It was good news. He wouldn't be acquiescing if he was *completely* against the idea of letting Evelyn stay put.

And once they had sorted it out, whatever the conclusion, she would hang around for another week maybe—make sure Evelyn was fine—and then return to Hawaii.

And the weird, unsettled feeling afflicting her would, thankfully, be gone.

CHAPTER THREE

It was very different here, Gabriel thought as he paused to look at the cottage tucked away amidst the trees. Where his mansion looked out to a sea of vines undulating towards a distant horizon, here, tucked away from the vineyards, the trees had been allowed to grow unchecked. It was the difference between order and a certain pleasing wildness. Flowers bloomed and the fading sun glinted through the trees, casting shadows in the undergrowth.

Gabriel had not ventured out here at all. He'd had no interest in it. His focus had been exclusively on the vineyards. He'd known about the cottage, and of course on the few occasions when he'd made the trip to the house he had glanced towards the sprawling, endless wooded area at the back and admired the contrast in scenery. That had been roughly the extent of it, though.

Had he not decided to extend his acreage, he would not have been overly concerned about the cottage. It was a gap in his holdings, but he could afford gaps. Who cared whether an elderly lady owned a tiny bit of neighbouring land? Doubtless, the previous owners had never anticipated extending their holdings, so the cottage in its little plot, situated in the furthest reaches and well out of sight, would never have proved bothersome.

It certainly wouldn't have been to Gabriel had he not been more ambitious in wanting to expand the winery. Not only would it provide jobs in the community—which was something that had clearly not occurred to Izzy in her heated rush to overturn his plans—but it would also be another step in that onward march away from the blistering poverty of his childhood.

So, alas, needs must.

Still, he could see what Izzy had been talking about. The cottage was very sweet. White picket fence, winding path to front door, faded red roof. It was fairy-tale stuff and, holding his hand, Rosa was clearly of the same opinion.

In fact, she had been enchanted by the woods ever since they had set off in search of the cottage. She had talked non-stop. She wanted to do some tree-climbing, she told him. Could she explore the woods on her own? She was bored staying in all the time. Could he come swim in the pool with her? Go to the shops with her? Play her computer game with her?

Right now she was hopping from one foot to the other, bristling with excitement. She ran towards the cottage, a slight, tanned kid in a scrappy T-shirt and a pair of denim shorts and some trainers, because she hated dresses or anything girly.

Gabriel followed.

His work load was intense. Things were happening with a couple of massive deals on the other side of the pond. His instinct was simply to get an agency to find someone who could temporarily cover Bella's absence, but his ex-wife's nasty jibes about his preoccupation with work had struck a chord. He was gearing up to an almighty battle with Bianca in trying to prevent her from absconding to Italy with Rosa.

Gabriel hadn't been born yesterday. For all his staggering wealth, he knew that in a court of law a mother would take precedence, especially if it could be proved that the father was consumed with work to the exclusion of everything else. Never mind the fact that Rosa, his number-one priority, the only female in his life to hold his heart, was the *very* reason he put in the hours. He had thrown money at Bianca following their divorce. She wanted for nothing, yet she remained embittered enough to paint him in the darkest of lights.

There was nothing more dangerous than a woman scorned. Gabriel had long concluded that Bianca's pride had taken a beating. She had been the high-born Italian beauty of impeccable lineage. Her mother was a dowager with far-reaching influence, even though the woman was now nearly seventy.

He, on the other hand, had been the poor kid

made good. His parents had been in service and had lived in near penury. Bianca had been born and raised to be worshipped, yet he had failed to pander to her demands, had ignored her, had failed to be jealous of her increasing need to flirt with other men. He had committed the gravest of sins by not treating her as number one and the fact that he was 'just an upstart', as she had screamed at one point, had been the final humiliation for her.

The truth was that he had married in haste because she had become pregnant, a mistake he blamed himself for, even though he later discovered that she had deliberately stopped taking the pill. He had not loved her, not been in love with her. He had, in the end, been indifferent and she had increasingly recognised that and hated him for it.

Gabriel had no intention of allowing his vindictive ex-wife to remove his daughter from his orbit, not least because it would be easy for her to make Rosa pay for *his* sins. That unplanned pregnancy had endowed him with the most precious gift of his life and he had no intention of allowing Rosa to be taken to Tuscany and out of his jurisdiction. Not if he could help it.

And there was something else. Gabriel was aware that his focus should be entirely on Rosa. He knew all about the importance of family life. He had grown up with devoted parents who had bent over backwards for him. He was divorced but suddenly it felt as though he was being driven down a different road from the one he had spent the past few years walking.

Perhaps it was the removal of a nanny. Without Bella around, he would have to confront his own limitations. Maybe the escalating situation with his ex had also rammed home that single-handedly running an empire did not make for perfect parenting. Or maybe it was being here, under a vast and serene sky. Life here was so very different from the cut and thrust, his fast-paced life in New York, where slowing down for five minutes was a luxury he seldom enjoyed.

What had been planned as a functional visit to conclude the business of the cottage, which his people had been unable to do, had turned into...

Something quite unexpected.

And just like that he thought of Izzy—her long, curling white-blonde hair, the argumentative pout of her mouth, the fiery glare of those aquamarine eyes.

Unexpected indeed, Gabriel thought.

Ever one to find solutions to problems and to seize opportunities as they came his way, Gabriel began quickly walking towards the cottage, his mind engaged on a tangent hitherto not considered. Rosa was waiting impatiently and he smiled.

'I love this!'

She was grinning like a Cheshire cat and Gabriel grinned back at her.

'Who knows?' he murmured, squatting so that

he was on eye level with her. 'Maybe you'll see a lot more of this enchanted place than I thought...'

With all the doors open, Izzy heard the sound of the knocker loud and clear, even though she and Evelyn were sitting outside in the back garden enjoying the last of the sunshine before it dipped away into night.

She'd explained the outcome of her meeting with Gabriel. She had actually referred to it as a 'meeting', making sure that everything was kept on a purely business level. This, in an effort to dispel some of the disconcerting effect he had on her.

She'd made sure to stress that nothing had been decided but during the course of the afternoon, as they had had tea and waited for Gabriel to show up, she had realised with a sinking heart that the older woman's hopes had been raised to an unrealistic level.

'I can't wait to show him my garden, dear,' Evelyn had told her excitedly. 'He'll want to see that this patch of land is not and never will be a blot on the landscape! You know how much I love this house and this oasis, dear. I feel that once he sees that for himself, he'll realise that there's no need to gobble up my house and land! He'll realise that we can be perfect neighbours. I may be elderly but I'm fit as a fiddle and well able to look after my little patch!'

'He'll be in no doubt about that,' Izzy had said, tentatively repeating what she had now said half a dozen times about *taking nothing for granted*.

'He strikes me as a pretty ruthless kind of guy,' she had felt constrained to point out, as they'd made their way back into the house. 'Not a very pleasant man *at all*.' She had thought of all six-foot-something of smouldering masculine beauty and had shivered.

Now, as she pulled open the front door, Izzy hoped that Evelyn had listened to her and heard what she had tried to say.

She was prepped to hiss a warning to him that he should be *gentle* with Evelyn, because she wasn't as robust as she looked, but was immediately thrown off-course by the sight of Rosa, who smiled with pure joy as she looked up at her.

'Can you take me out to the back?' she asked, dropping Gabriel's hand and stepping forward towards Izzy. 'Is there an apple tree? Can you draw some more stuff for me? I should have brought my drawing pad.' She looked crestfallen. 'Dad, can we go back so that—'

'It's okay.' Izzy smiled. The dad might set her teeth on edge but his daughter was a poppet, she thought. She sneaked a glance towards Gabriel to find him looking thoughtfully at her. She hurriedly looked away and stooped down. 'I'm pretty sure I can rustle up some paper,' she said. 'And of course there's an apple tree! What cottage *doesn't* have an apple tree? And lots of plants and flowers and herbs and vegetables. I'll draw some cartoon pictures of them, if you like. You pick the vegetable and I'll turn it into whatever you want.'

'Excellent plan.'

Izzy glanced up at Gabriel's deep voice to find him stepping around her into the house and introducing himself to Evelyn. Gone was the cool, unyielding face he had shown Izzy. In its place was a smile of such easy charm that she had to blink to make sure her eyes weren't playing tricks on her.

They weren't. The tenor of his voice matched the twinkle in his dark eyes as he began chatting to Evelyn.

'What a stunning location… The cottage is charming… Tell me about all those photos… Yes, I'm sure the garden is as beautiful as the cottage…'

He now turned to Izzy, his smile still in place, although the expression in his eyes informed her that he wasn't about to brook any staging of a protest at this point.

'Why don't you take charge of Rosa for a while? Give me an opportunity to talk to Evelyn in private.'

Evelyn, Izzy noted with dismay, seemed to be lapping up Gabriel's superficial charm. Her eyes were bright, her smile was broad and she was positively blushing with pleasure as he continued to lay it on thick, chatting winningly while managing to propel her back into the house and out in the direction of the garden.

Evelyn was bustling towards the kitchen, chirpily telling him about some home-made lemonade and carrot cake. Izzy tried to catch his eye but he was having none of it, instead choosing to give his daughter the go-ahead to explore outside for as long as she wanted.

'Absolutely no hurry.' He finally looked at Izzy as he vaulted upright, so shockingly sexy in some faded jeans and a black polo shirt that he took her breath away.

Izzy scowled, deprived of any opportunity to tell him what he should and shouldn't say to Evelyn, because there was no way she would allow him to offend the older woman in any way. Rosa was impatiently waiting to go outside and, as far as chaperones went, she was the best he could have hoped for, silencing all the warning protests bubbling up inside Izzy. When he grinned with slow, lazy deliberation, she realised that he knew exactly what was going through her head.

But what could she say when Rosa looked up between them, keen to play explorer out in the garden?

For the next hour and a half, while Gabriel was closeted away in the cosy sitting room with Evelyn, Izzy entertained his daughter. Which was not hard work, she had to admit because, the better acquainted she got with the child, the more she appreciated just how smart and curious the little girl was.

Notwithstanding, half of her was preoccupied with what Gabriel and Evelyn could possibly be talking about for such a long time. She was far from reassured when, having retreated to the kitchen table with Rosa so that part two of the entertainment programme—drawing—could be completed, she heard the sitting-room door open and within minutes Evelyn was framed in the doorway, beaming.

Gabriel towered behind her, his face revealing nothing at all.

'Time to go, Rosa.'

Rosa debated for a couple of seconds whether she was ready to leave, but then reluctantly began gathering up the sheets of paper while Izzy stood up, stretched and likewise mentally debated what she should do now.

She was spared the decision making when Gabriel said in the sort of voice that assumed compliance, 'Why don't you accompany me back to the house, Izzy? You and I can have a chat.'

'Evelyn and I might…want to catch up…' Izzy glanced at Evelyn, who *winked*.

'You run along with Gabriel, dear, and we can talk tomorrow.'

As Rosa began clattering with the pencils Izzy had managed to locate in a kitchen drawer, and shuffling the bits of paper so that she could show them to Gabriel, Evelyn took Izzy to one side and said *sotto voce*, 'What a *lovely* man, dear. I don't know why I got myself so worked up about this whole thing. He seems very *understanding*.'

'Evelyn…'

'Now hush, dear. I know you went through that

rough time, but not all men are the same, and Gabriel has been more than sympathetic to what I've been going through. The worry…' She shook her head and Izzy saw tears of relief in the older woman's eyes.

She groaned inwardly because the person Evelyn was describing bore no resemblance to the person Izzy had met yesterday, and Izzy was willing to bet that her version was much closer to the truth.

But she refrained from saying anything because she couldn't bear to see the optimistic light in Evelyn's eyes snuffed out.

She also refrained from saying anything as they walked back to the big house. The evening had brought a coolness to the air and, in her T-shirt and short skirt, Izzy felt a relief when that massive front door was pushed open and she stepped past Gabriel into the warmth.

He wanted to chat. It felt ominous, even though there was nothing in his demeanour to indicate any such thing.

'I'll settle Rosa.' He turned to her, addressing her directly for the first time since leaving the cottage. 'Why don't you wait for me in the kitchen? Help yourself to anything you like. This is wine-growing country. It would be a shame not to have a glass. There is some excellent Chardonnay in the fridge.'

He swung round before she could inform him that she had no intention of having anything to drink, repeating the mantra of the day before.

But once in the kitchen Izzy decided that a glass

wouldn't do any harm. Indeed, she felt it might numb her senses to his overpowering appeal and the threat it posed to her attempts at composure.

She was rigid with tension by the time he strolled into the kitchen.

'You were with Evelyn a long time.' She said what had been feverishly playing on her mind ever since they had begun walking back to his house. With Rosa between them chatting non-stop, there had been no opportunity to find out what he and the older woman had discussed and all Izzy's worries had had ample time to bloom.

Gabriel shot her a veiled look but didn't say anything, preferring to help himself to a glass of wine, the same wine now in front of Izzy, as yet untouched.

He took his time before he replied, leaving her to stew for a few minutes, then sat down opposite her, his head tilted to one side, as though considering what he should say next and how.

'There was a lot to talk about,' Gabriel concurred. 'It was a mistake to delegate this situation to one of my employees. I'm big enough to recognise that I should have sorted this business out myself. I made a mistake sending in the boys to do a man's job.' He shrugged and sipped his wine while he continued to look at her over the rim of his glass.

'And has it been sorted?' The million-dollar question, which was answered in full when he remained noticeably silent in response. 'Evelyn is over the moon!' Izzy exploded angrily. How could he just *sit there*, having met Evelyn, having seen with his own eyes how emotionally dependent she was on the only place she had ever really called home? 'She really thinks that she's going to be allowed to get on with her life in the cottage! She really thinks that you're one of the good guys.'

'And you've already made your mind up that I'm not.'

'Why did you encourage her to think that everything was going to be all right if you had no intention of…of…?'

'You're looking at this through the wrong set of lenses.'

'I'm leaving!'

'No,' Gabriel said shortly. 'You're not. Sit back down, finish the glass of wine and we can discuss this thorny situation.'

'You can't tell me what to do!'

'No. I can't. What I *can* say, however, is that the option I am presenting makes sense and is the right course of action given the circumstances. I am far from being a monster, which you would see if you would just drop the emotionalism for five seconds.' Their eyes tangled and Izzy shot him a scorching look from under her lashes.

'Some things can't just be looked at with pure common sense. Some things are *invested* with emotion. It's just that *you*,' she returned without blinking an eye, 'Can't see that because *you* are as cold as ice!'

'Not always…' Gabriel murmured. Their eyes tangled and just like that the atmosphere between them shifted. Hot colour rose to her cheeks and suddenly the room felt way too stifling and way too small, the walls closing in as he continued to look at her with lazy, hooded eyes. She was clutching the sides of her chair so that her knuckles were white and leaning ever so slightly forward, unable to drag her gaze away from his lean, darkly handsome face.

He was the first to break eye contact. 'It's not a simple case of black and white.' He raked his fingers through his hair and sighed impatiently. 'I'm not a charitable organisation, neither am I Father Christmas. I don't intend to reside here permanently, nor am I qualified to manage these vineyards the way they deserve to be managed. The guy currently in charge here is renting a lodge in the town. Not ideal. He needs help. The staff, too, will have to be accommodated some distance away, simply because the cottage is out of bounds as a housing compound.'

'If you're not going to be here, why can't you use this place for them? It's big enough.'

'Not the point. I want to increase production and I'll need to buy up what's beyond the cottage. There will be infringement to a large degree on your friend's privacy.'

'And you explained all of that to her?'

'I…tried,' Gabriel said heavily.

'Well,' Izzy couldn't resist sniping with heavy sarcasm, 'You obviously failed, because Evelyn thinks it's all over bar the shouting, that she's going to be safe where she is.'

'What is her story? Why has she never thought of moving? She's on her own. Surely it's lonely being stuck out here? Wouldn't she rather be close to her friends? Her…whatever it is she does to occupy her time? Leisure activities? I know she devotes a considerable amount of time to her vegetables and the garden, and it seems she's an active member of the local gardening society, but are there other hobbies she would want to pursue that require her to be closer to the centre of the town?'

'Evelyn is…' Izzy breathed in deeply. 'Her entire life was devoted to the family she used to work for. They lived in this house, you see, and they actually bequeathed her the cottage because she was more than just a nanny. She was a family friend.'

'What family?' He frowned. 'I had no idea the family I bought this place from had children. Or a nanny.'

'I believe the place was bought and sold a couple of times before it became yours.'

Silence fell. Izzy fiddled with the stem of the glass and then nervously swallowed far too much of the golden wine and winced.

Gabriel looked at her, eyes narrowed, without saying a word. Her tone of voice. Her face, that delicate blush…

Had he ever met any woman whose face revealed

so much? She was feisty and spirited and wasn't afraid of speaking her mind, but there was also a blushing ingenuousness about her that fascinated him.

Right now, her expressive face was leading him to conclusions that all seemed to tie together and make sense of her presence in the area, as they did her determination to defend Evelyn against the Big Bad Wolf.

'This family you're talking about…' He reached forward, elbow on the table, and gently hooked his finger under her chin so that she was looking at him. On the periphery of his mind, he was aware that her skin was very soft and satiny smooth, and he had to resist the urge to cup the side of her face with his hand, to stroke her cheek, to touch her lips with his thumb. He dropped his hand and sat back.

Izzy looked away and then twirled her hair in her hands, sifting her fingers through its length.

'Evelyn used to work for my grandparents. It's no big secret. She was my mother's nanny and remained with the family until the day they sold the place and moved away when my grandfather became ill. They needed somewhere smaller. They wanted to take Evelyn with them, but she wanted to remain in the area, and so they gave her the cottage and the land around it as a measure of thanking her for her service over the years.'

'Your family used to live here?'

'It's no big deal, like I said.'

No big deal? Gabriel thought. He had built an image in his head of fetching innocence, an ingenuousness that was refreshing. But of course, he'd been wildly off-target. If her grandparents had owned this property and the vineyards that went with it, they would not have been scraping the barrel to find food. He might have extended the original property and dragged it out of disrepair, because the years and the people before him had been unable to keep the place going, but even so...

The ethereal blonde with the big blue eyes was a trust-fund kid, and didn't he know all about trust-fund kids? You couldn't trust them as far as you could throw them because the assumption that they would get what they wanted was woven into their DNA. His ex had taught him a lot when it came to that particular subject. He might not have been the perfect husband, but she'd been able to trust him, and he'd mistakenly thought the same until she'd let him down in the biggest way possible. So, rich kids? Thanks, but no thanks.

Yet he had to concede that his daughter had taken a liking to this woman. In fact, Rosa had been unable to talk about anything else but the cottage, the apple tree and the blonde's amazing talent at drawing.

'My mother was an only child,' Izzy volunteered reluctantly. 'She talked a lot about Nanny Scott.'

'*Talked* about?'

'My mother died twelve years ago,' Izzy said shortly. 'I was ten at the time.'

'Twelve years ago,' he murmured. 'You were only a child. I'm sorry.'

She nodded and lowered her eyes.

In the brief, intervening silence, Gabriel couldn't help but marvel that his usually impeccable judgement had been flawed in this instance.

His own bitter experience of what a woman born into money could be like had been a deep learning curve. Wealthy men were often suspicious of gold-diggers, but as far as Gabriel was concerned with a gold-digger you knew where you stood. You had money, they wanted it and, if you chose to comply, then you did so with eyes wide open. But rich young things came with all sorts of hidden dangers and, whilst the rational part of him could concede that, rich or poor, no two people were ever the same, he still responded to trust-fund babes with a primal, gut reaction that had its roots in his own bitter, personal experience.

'So your purpose in coming here was to…?'

'See where my mum grew up.'

'And you decided to go one step further and fight Evelyn's corner when she told you about the cottage. Did you think that you would have a chat with me and I'd concede defeat?' He wondered whether a privileged background had inured her against failure. In his steady climb up the greasy pole, it had become apparent that there was a yawning gap between the way those born into money approached life and those who had grown up without it.

Moneyed people, whether they deserved it or not, whether they were clever or not or gifted or not, assumed that success was their due.

He watched her narrowly, making assumptions now that had not been made before.

'No, of course not.'

'Here's the thing.' He leaned forward and looked at her seriously. 'I am prepared to at least review the situation.'

'Really?'

'I hadn't expected to find myself persuaded into thinking any more deeply about your friend and her living here next to my land, but she is clearly dependent on the cottage because, as you have explained, it has been her home for very many years…'

'And of course,' Izzy jumped in with enthusiasm, 'The older you get, the more stuck in your ways you become and the less willing you are to have any kind of change in your life.'

'That's as may be.' Gabriel had listened and taken on board what the older woman had had to say, but he had manoeuvred the conversation to exploring various options should they arise. He had encouraged her to talk about her friends in the town, and had made sure to point out how vital it was for people to have friends or family close by when old age began setting in. While she had waxed lyrical about the garden, and the joys of growing her own vegetables, he had quietly inserted the suggestion that some other properties came with outside space cry-ing out for someone with green fingers, that the garden she maintained did not necessarily have to be the last one she ever maintained.

Far from threatening, he had charmed and had left her with things to think about. He had planted seeds. As a talented gardener, he felt that she would appreciate the effort.

Gabriel had no intention of abandoning his plans but, for once, he was not going to go for the jugular. He'd liked the woman. He would gently guide her in the direction he wished her to take and he had no hesitation that she would go exactly where directed.

But before he got there…

'I have a proposition for you,' he said, relaxing and watching Izzy closely.

'What is it?'

'You're hell-bent on saving your friend from the horror of having to sell the cottage for an unbelievably and unrealistically generous sum of money.' He watched as predictably she stiffened, sitting up straighter, her mouth pursing in immediate rejection of what he had said. And what a very nice mouth she had, Gabriel thought absently. Spoiled brat she undoubtedly was, despite outward appearances, but what an extremely fetching and addictively watchable spoiled brat.

Izzy opened her mouth to argue and he stifled the protest on her lips with a dismissive wave of his hand.

'I'm in no mood to start a pointless debate about

whether my offer is generous or not. Back to my proposition.'

'You're so arrogant,' Izzy said.

'I know. You'd be amazed at how few women have ever complained about that trait before.'

'And conceited.'

'The two often go hand in hand.' He reluctantly smiled. Spoiled brat or not, no one had entertained him quite as much in recent times. 'I'm prepared to, at least, consider your friend's dilemma but in return you have to do something for me.'

'What?' Izzy asked cautiously.

'I'm here without a nanny and there are times when it is impossible for me to focus entirely on entertaining Rosa because I have work to do.'

'You want me to babysit her now and again?'

'Rather more than that. I want you to take over where Bella left off. There's no chance she'll be out of hospital any time soon and if I am to stay here, mulling things over about the cottage, possibly having further chats with Evelyn…'

'Provided I look after Rosa because you can't see your way to having a couple of weeks away from your work…'

Gabriel frowned but decided not to take issue with that blatantly provocative remark. 'You would have to live in. It's more convenient, especially if I need to return to New York for anything. I would need you to be on hand.'

'In other words,' Izzy said slowly, 'You're blackmailing me. You'll think about backing off if I help you out with Rosa. Why don't you just hire someone for a week or so?'

Gabriel thought of Bianca and the open airwaves between Bella and her. The last thing he needed was to give his ex-wife ammunition that she would cheerfully use against him in a court of law.

Izzy was not a nanny. She was a friend helping out now and again.

'My daughter is really taken with you,' Gabriel said truthfully. 'I very much doubt that any nanny would be able to slide seamlessly into Rosa's life for such a short space of time, whereas you…' She wasn't qualified, yet there was something about her he instinctively trusted, and the fact that his daughter was bowled over by her spoke volumes. She had a certain sweetness in her that was at odds with her wealthy background and he was willing to concede that she might not quite fit the one-dimensional mould he had been quite happy to slot her into.

'I… I might have other things to do… Plans for filling my time while I'm here…'

'No, you don't. A person with plans doesn't decide to remain in one place on a whim.'

'Don't tell me what I might or might not have planned!'

'It's a simple question, Izzy, a simple deal. Do you take it or not?'

CHAPTER FOUR

IZZY ARRIVED THE following morning with all her clothes stuffed into the Louis Vuitton suitcase she had brought along with her when she had fled Hawaii.

The mansion looked all the more imposing now that she was going to be moving in. When Gabriel had first put his proposition forward, just for a second Izzy had thought that he had been kidding. She'd clocked quickly enough that he was deadly serious.

He had laid it on thick with the charm for Evelyn's benefit and the older woman had fallen for it hook, line and sinker.

She had misguidedly believed that his easy manner, that way he had of looking as though he was really listening and utterly focused, meant that he was going to allow her to stay where she was without forcing her out by fair means or foul. He had been soothing and reassuring and she taken the wrong message from his demeanour.

Izzy had arrived at an altogether different interpretation of events and one she knew to be far closer to reality.

He was fattening Evelyn up for the kill. Let her bask in the contentment of thinking she was safe, and the second he told her what life would look like when the tractors moved in she would have no fight left and would collapse without a struggle.

That said…there was the slimmest chance that she was wrong, the vaguest possibility that he really was going to consider his options. So she felt that she could not reject his offer out of hand. Maybe, living under the same roof, she might even be able to employ some powers of persuasion to make him see sense, to steer him away from pursuing yet another unnecessary addition to his portfolio.

Now, as she rang the doorbell, she felt her stomach muscles tighten at the prospect of living with the man, sharing space with him, being *swamped* twenty-four-seven by his suffocating personality.

Izzy was banking down a rising tide of belated panic when the front door was pulled open, but thankfully not by Gabriel. Marie, the young housekeeper, had a tea towel slung over her shoulder and her hair was pulled back with a scarf. She was pink faced but smiling, and behind her Rosa was hopping from one foot to the other.

'She's been waiting for the past hour,' Marie confided. 'I could barely get the cleaning done because she's been tagging along behind me telling me about all the stuff you two are going to be doing.'

'Well, I'll have to get rid of this bag first…' Izzy smiled at Rosa, who immediately took charge as only a child can do. She flew up the stairs, breathlessly pointing out things along the way, and the question uppermost in Izzy's head concerning the whereabouts of Gabriel was lost in the excitement of her arrival.

She relaxed, the panic subsided and the day progressed, filled with an agenda of fast-paced activities inspired by an active and enthusiastic six-year-old with reserves of energy that beggared belief.

Izzy had almost forgotten her dread of being in the same house as Gabriel until, at a little after six and after an enjoyable visit to the cottage—where Evelyn had come alive in Rosa's company—they both wearily returned to the house to find Gabriel in the kitchen, drink in one hand, waiting for them.

In low-slung, faded jeans, a white T-shirt and bare feet, he looked sinfully sexy and horribly tempting, and Izzy stopped dead in her tracks as her mouth dried and her brain fogged over.

Their eyes met over Rosa's head and he raised his eyebrows, which brought her sharply back down to earth.

'I must just get changed.' She did a sweeping gesture to encompass her khaki shorts and T-shirt. 'I'll leave you two to catch up on the day.'

She fled, straight up to the room she had been assigned.

Her heart was beating like a sledgehammer. She stared out of the window, gathering her composure. It was a peaceful sight. Manicured grounds, an infinity pool and the sweeping expanse of vineyards in the distance all set under a vast sky. There was a feel of cowboy territory, with the purple haze of the mountains far away on the horizon. She looked away and headed for the *en suite*.

This, she told herself, was not going to do. She was not going to let herself get flustered every time she laid eyes on the man. She was not going to let him see the sort of unwelcome effect he had on her. She'd committed to this job, though it couldn't be called a job, because when he'd offered to pay her she'd firmly refused. She wasn't going to be undermined by a swirl of emotion that had no place inside her.

She was going to stop noticing the way he looked if it killed her. The truth was, she was emphatically *not* attracted to men like Gabriel Ricci. He wasn't easygoing and he wasn't fun-loving. He was yet another example of a rich financier who put money above everything else. Never having been allowed to be a rebel, part of her knew that her aversion to ambitious, ruthless workaholics was her way of sticking two fingers up at her domineering older brother and the way he had controlled her life.

The best thing she could do would be to ignore Gabriel's impact and instead focus on trying to get him to change his mind about the cottage. He'd told her that he was a guy who never changed direction but even the most unlikely people changed direction.

Look at Max! Who would ever have thought that her work-orientated, driven older brother, so accustomed to running her life, would have found it in himself to understand where she'd been coming from with the hotel? Would have sympathised with the whole Jefferson saga and held off on ferrying her back to Hawaii to pick up where she had left off? Just went to show that there was no such thing as someone never changing direction. Given the circumstances with Evelyn, it was a fortifying conclusion.

Izzy returned to the kitchen, freshly showered and in soft grey trousers and a loose, pale-grey T-shirt. She had tied her hair back into a braid, but her hair was so curly that it refused to obey the rules, and she knew that the neat look she was aiming for was a borderline failure.

Gabriel was nowhere to be seen, and for a hopeful moment she wondered whether he had taken himself back off to work. But, just as she was about to start exploring the kitchen with relative confidence that she wouldn't be interrupted, she heard footsteps and then there he was, framed in the doorway, still in those faded jeans and that white T-shirt, still barefoot.

She could feel every muscle in her body tense and she had to make an effort to breathe evenly.

'Is…is Rosa asleep?'

'At last. She was very over-excited.' He strolled towards the fridge, took out a bottle of water and drank from it, before turning to her.

'I…er…' Izzy was uncertain as to how this time of the evening would evolve. 'If you don't mind, I'll just head upstairs…'

'Marie prepares food every day while we're in residence. Join me.'

'I don't mind taking my food upstairs. I'm not sure how you spend the evenings once Rosa is asleep, but I wouldn't want to interrupt your pattern.'

Izzy knew that this was precisely how she should *not* be acting but he made her so jittery that she couldn't think straight in his presence. Yet she needed to. She needed to hammer home her point of view or else why was she here? She couldn't afford to dither and hope that he did the right thing off his own bat. She took a deep breath and risked a smile. 'Except I would say that your pattern's probably really disrupted already with Rosa's nanny lying on a hospital bed. Can I ask something?'

She watched as he peered inside the frying pan, tidily covered on the stove, and then the fridge, from which he retrieved a perfectly prepared salad under cling film. He fetched plates from a cupboard. He still hadn't said anything although, once plates wer on the table, along with the opened bottle of wine, he quirked an eyebrow and said wryly, 'Could I stop you?'

'Why do you employ a nanny that your daughter dislikes?'

'Is that what Rosa has told you?'

Izzy nodded. This was really none of her business because whether Rosa liked her nanny or not was beside the point. The woman would recover, return to work and Izzy would be off, whether she succeeded in changing Gabriel's mind or not. They were all ships passing in the night so curiosity was a waste of time.

Still…the more she saw of the little girl, the more she liked her, and she was deeply curious as to the strange set-up with Bella.

And, if she were to be completely honest with herself, the distant set-up Rosa had with her mother—who, from all accounts, spent an awful lot of time socialising, shopping and pampering herself—concerned her. Izzy vaguely knew, from conversations with James over the years, that her own mother had been absent for much of her brothers' formative years—having dispatched both James and Max to boarding schools practically from the time they'd taken their first steps—but for her, things had been different.

Her memories were much rosier. Her mother had treated her like a doll, dressing her up and letting her experiment with her make-up, shoes and clothes. Izzy had known that her parents were both away a lot, compared to the parents of all her friends, but when they'd been around her mother had delighted in doing all sorts of mother-and-daughter things with her.

'I adore having a little girl,' she had once sighed, when Izzy had been turning eight, and that passing comment had thrilled her to the bone.

And then, in a heartbeat, both her parents were gone and she was left with a great empty space inside her, even though people had rallied around. And of course both her brothers had taken her under their wing and done their utmost to numb the shock and pain. That great, empty space had never really been filled. It had sat right alongside her every step of the way as she had moved from childhood into adolescence and then into adulthood.

Izzy thought it sad that Rosa's passing remarks about her mother were so lacking in affection. Of course, she knew that it might just be the nonchalance of a child, but there were so few stories she shared that seemed special. And could she actually be telling the truth when she'd flippantly let slip that she was taken out of school quite often and taught by Bella on the move, to accommodate her mother's love of travelling to far-flung places?

With a grim nanny in the equation, however competent she might technically be, it all seemed desperately sad.

'It's none of my business,' she said when he failed to answer. 'Whatever Marie has cooked, it smells delicious. Is this your routine when you're here? She cooks for you and you have your dinner on your own?'

'It's my routine wherever in the world I happen

to be,' Gabriel responded drily. 'Unless, which is more often the case, I go out to eat.'

He looked at her with a hooded expression. This was a novel experience for him and normal rules did not apply. What else had Rosa said to her? He was well aware that Izzy was here under duress and nursing some notion that he might be prepared to back down on his plans for the cottage.

He wasn't concerned about using her. He had met very many rich young things, and the one thing he knew for sure about all of them was that they were hard as nails. Whatever the guise. Wealth created a veneer, made you think that you could take what you wanted without conscience. Izzy might appear to be as pure as the driven snow but he would bet his life that she was tough as old boots. She probably thought that she could change his mind because she would have been conditioned to expect to get her own way in most situations. The overriding power of his past experience was a force that locked the door on trust.

His eyes drifted to her full pink mouth, that tangle of blonde hair and the pure cornflower blue of her big, wide eyes. Sexy as hell, he thought, and no doubt as experienced as any woman he had ever slept with, even though she might not give off the same vibes.

Just thinking about her in that way sent a rush of hot blood straight down to his groin and he shifted uncomfortably, turning away for a moment to busy himself doing something with whatever Marie had cooked—some kind of chicken dish. He was back to his usual cool when he strolled to the table, waving down her offer to help as he deposited the salad, cutlery and then the pan, not bothering to decant its contents.

Gabriel had suspected for some time that Bianca played fast and loose with the parenting process, although there was no way he would ever put his daughter in the position of having to provide answers to his questions.

His ex-wife was very good when it came to laying down ground rules, only to break them. She was very good when it came to blatantly defying the court order on shared custody, just keeping on the right side of his tipping point. She knew how to use his workaholic's schedule against him, just as she knew that the women he dated, the relationships that never matured into anything permanent, put him at a distinct disadvantage when it came to fighting her in a court of law for more custody of Rosa. She knew his weaknesses and she knew how to exploit them. And Bella could always be relied upon to ferry news back to her.

He looked under his lashes at the blonde helping herself to what seemed a vast amount of food for someone who weighed nothing. Momentarily distracted, he watched as she heaped her plate, before raising apologetic eyes to him.

'I'm hungrier than I thought,' she muttered.

'A woman with a hearty appetite. That's a first for me. Tell me what you did today with Rosa.'

Gabriel listened intently while she went through the events of her day with his daughter. He relaxed because, although he only had a scant idea of what life might be like for Rosa with his ex-wife, he knew what it was like with Bella and it warmed him to hear an account of what had been quite a different day for his daughter with Izzy.

His jaw hardened. He had been patient for a very long time with Bianca. Now he had the scent of payback in the air because, if his ex could play dirty, then he could return the favour if there was any suspicion that her parenting was below par.

The information he would never have prised from his daughter now hovered tantalisingly within reach because it was apparent that Rosa was building a close and confiding relationship with the woman opposite him tucking into her food with gusto. He thought that his daughter, like any other child her age, would be good at unconditionally giving affection to someone they immediately took a liking to.

'You asked about Bella,' he introduced when there was a lull in the conversation.

Dinner at an end, he pushed aside his plate, shoved back his chair and relaxed, linking his fingers on his stomach and watching her with lazy interest.

She looked so damned *fresh*. She looked like what he had first thought her to be—someone without the

tiresome airs and graces that came with privilege…
someone not yet cynical enough to think that money
bought everything. He dropped his eyes and recalled
the very expensive Louis Vuitton case that had ac-
companied her into his house. He had glimpsed her
earlier from the window of the room he currently
used as his office as she had stepped out of her taxi.

'You don't have to answer,' Izzy shrugged once
again, and regretfully closed her knife and fork.

'Bella is a relative of my ex-wife,' Gabriel expanded, ignoring the uneasy tug inside him at this
innocuous exchange of information. So unaccus-
tomed was he to sharing any aspect of his private
life with anyone, the admission felt oddly disconcerting. It felt like a tacit admission of *trust,* and yet
it surely couldn't be? Trust was something that had
been taken from him through those bitter years when
he had discovered just how fragile it was.

'So I guess you had to employ her if your…ex-
wife…asked,' Izzy mused sympathetically. 'It's
tempting to give jobs to people you're related to.'

'I wouldn't have, given half a chance,' Gabriel
grated. 'But unfortunately my ex-wife can be vindictive and is fond of playing games.' He looked away
briefly. 'Including those that use Rosa as a pawn.'

'I'm sorry,' Izzy said, aghast and not hiding it. She
felt a warm, protective rush towards her little charge
and knew that it was because there was a meeting of
mutual ground here. A daughter without her mother,

whatever the reasons behind it might be, was a child set up to experience loss. She should know.

'Don't be. As you've said, this is hardly your concern.' He stood up and stretched before removing the crockery to the sink, where he proceeded haphazardly to stack the lot at the side. 'Bella's methods are draconian when applied to a six-year-old, which is why Rosa is so rebellious. She may do everything by the book but, when it comes to kids, that's not always the right way.'

'Couldn't you talk to your wife, your *ex*-wife, about that? It doesn't matter how vindictive she is, surely the main thing is Rosa's happiness?'

'In an ideal world, I would.' Gabriel said wryly. 'Unfortunately, the world is rarely ideal. I am just pleased that my daughter is having fun with you.'

'I'm not engaging her in any educational activities, though…'

'You mean like Bella?'

'There is a timetable from the sounds of it, and quite a gruelling one. No subject is left unexplored, even during the holidays.' She relaxed and grinned. That glass of wine had taken the edge off her nervous tension, as had the fact that they were on neutral territory, discussing something other than the contentious issue of the cottage. 'I guess I would be able to do homework with her, but I wouldn't enjoy it. I did business studies at university but…'

Gabriel tilted his head to one side. 'But…?'

'But it was the wrong choice,' Izzy mumbled.

'Why?'

Izzy shrugged and swept her hair over one shoulder, a nervous gesture, because she needed to do something with her hands. 'I'm happy to keep to my side of the bargain.' She changed the subject. 'But will you really consider backing down on the business with the cottage? At least try and stand back and see it from a different perspective?'

'Of course,' Gabriel lied magnanimously.

Her non-answer to his question intrigued him. It was easy to pigeonhole rich young women because he personally had had a great deal of experience with them. Hell, he'd made the colossal mistake of marrying one of them!

Rich young women, he had found over the years, enjoyed talking about themselves and were always happy to fill in the blanks with minimum encouragement from him.

He had no problem with that. Bianca had put him off the institution of marriage for good. The experience had also taught him something very valuable about himself: he would always put work ahead of everyone and everything, with the exception of his daughter. Even so, with some guilt he knew that there was more he could do with her.

But for women? They would always take a back seat. He had grown up on the wrong side of the tracks and knew, from experience, just how tough life could be when you could barely afford to put food on your plate. His parents had worked their fingers to the bone, had done their best for him, but still they had been suffocated by a society that only recognised people with money. Their ambition had been to give him the opportunity to escape the trap into which they had been born and there was no way he had ever had any intention of disappointing on that front.

Poverty and scraping by? Bowing and taking orders from someone else who happened to have money even if they weren't any smarter? No way. Somewhere along the line, Gabriel knew that he had traded emotions for hard-headed ambition and he was not regretful about the trade-off.

It just meant that he knew exactly where women slotted into his life, and it had to be said that the hard-nosed rich young things he dated suited him. He wasn't in the market for emotional attachment but he was more than happy to show them a good time. When he thought of those other women out there, the sort of women he knew his parents desperately hoped he would meet, he felt a shiver run down his spine. Those women—with high hopes and expectations, vulnerable and waiting to be hurt, trusting and keen for their happy-ever-afters with a domesticated husband and kids running around—were women to be avoided at all costs. He just didn't have what it took to give any of that to them and he was brutally realistic about those shortcomings.

The doe-eyed beauty with the rich parents intrigued him and against all odds she stirred a certain amount of curiosity just because she was different from the pack, even though she did, indeed, come from the same stable.

And if he gained her trust…if she chose to confide in him any shortcomings that might be mentioned in connection with his ex-wife…then who was he not to use that information to his advantage?

It would certainly make a change, bearing in mind he had been on the back foot with Bianca ever since their acrimonious divorce.

'I've spoken to the hospital,' he said smoothly. 'They anticipate at least two weeks. It would seem that Bella has some underlying health issues that might hamper a speedy recovery.'

'Two weeks?'

'Of course, I can't tie you to a post and make you stay…but you have to appreciate that such a major rethink isn't something that can be effected in a handful of days. A considerable amount of money is involved, not to mention the man hours that have gone into researching the feasibility of such a massive addition to the vineyards I currently own.'

Izzy lowered her eyes then looked at him. 'Two weeks,' she said. 'At the end of that, if you're still *considering the options*, then I'll know that you have no intention of changing your plans.'

* * *

Three days after Izzy had moved in, Evelyn had worriedly told her that she was sure she had spotted someone *out there* doing *something*.

'I thought everything was going to be all right,' she had said anxiously. It had surprised Izzy that, even though doubts were beginning to form in the older woman's head, she still insisted on clinging to the false belief that Gabriel—*such a lovely man*—wouldn't do anything underhand.

That very evening—after she had had her shower and delivered Rosa to her father for what had become an evening ritual, whereby he bonded with his daughter for an hour or so before she went to bed—Izzy headed to the kitchen to wait for him.

Disconcertingly, this too had become something of a ritual. How? She had braced herself for awkward encounters where she either avoided him or else tried to pin him down to make some kind of decision. Instead, she had been lulled into conversing about what she and Rosa had done during the day. He asked so many questions and, after a glass of wine, which was something else she had become accustomed to, she found that chatting to him and answering those questions eclipsed all her good intentions when it came to pressing him for an answer about the cottage.

She was uneasily aware that she was probably being used because he needed someone on tap for Rosa while he was working during the day, and he was right—a temporary nanny would have taken far too much breaking in for such a short period of time.

She grew fonder of the child by the day but she was shrewd enough to know that her adorable little charge was precociously clever and very much had a mind of her own.

Izzy had rehearsed her line of attack and, the minute he entered the kitchen, she said without beating around the bush, 'Evelyn said that she saw someone in the neighbouring vineyards and he seemed to be someone official.'

She gritted her teeth together, impatiently waiting for him to reply, watching as he peered into the oven to see what was there. Not for the first time, she marvelled at just how lacking in interest he seemed to be when it came to cooking for himself.

'Well?' she asked, resisting the urge to snap.

'Things that have been set in motion,' Gabriel countered smoothly as he strolled towards the kitchen table and sat down next to her, swivelling the chair so that he was facing her directly, 'Are continuing at the moment. Various experts were booked to inspect the vineyards I planned on buying quite some time ago. I'm sorry to disappoint you, but I don't intend to issue full-scale cancellation orders on the off chance that I may not go ahead with the project.'

'I'll convey the message to Evelyn,' Izzy said stiffly. 'I'm sure she'll be over the moon that the trust she had in you was completely misplaced. I've suddenly lost my appetite. I think I'll retire for the evening now.'

'Any messages about what I do with my land or any land I might be considering buying,' Gabriel informed her with steely determination, 'Will be conveyed by me.'

'What difference does it make?' Izzy tilted her chin at a belligerent angle and glared.

'You're very used to getting what you want in life, aren't you?' he returned softly.

Izzy floundered. This was a question she had not been expecting and the way in which it was delivered, coolly and with derision, sent a shiver racing down her spine.

'What makes you say that?'

'Izzy, you're a rich young woman, and I'll wager that you assumed, deep down, that you would get what you wanted, and what you wanted was for me to back-pedal on this deal whatever the financial fallout for me.'

'That's not true!' Tears pricked the back of her eyes and she felt herself break out in a light film of nervous perspiration. 'How dare you pretend to know what sort of person I am?'

'I am an excellent judge of people,' Gabriel countered without batting an eye. 'Of course, I might be wrong…' He shrugged his broad shoulders with just the sort of dismissive nonchalance that left Izzy in no doubt that he believed himself to be absolutely right.

'Well, you *are* wrong.' She stood up, flinging the chair back, her cheeks bright-red with defiance. 'I have *never* gone through life expecting *anything*!' She spun round on her heels and headed for the door, but then she stopped, her breath coming in fast bursts. He wasn't stopping her, and yet her feet refused to propel her out of the kitchen, because this was a conversation that seemed to need an ending. She could *feel* him behind her and her breathing quickened.

He could be…so…*arrogant* and yet she was ashamed to admit that she had been charmed by him over the past few days, had dropped her defences and fallen under some kind of crazy spell.

More fool her.

'Haven't you?'

Izzy slowly turned round and pressed herself against the door in a desperate effort at distancing him, although he was so close… Her throat tightened in an instant, horrifying response to his proximity.

With devastating clarity, she realised that she had spent the past few evenings not just relaxing in his company, not just dropping the antagonism that she had originally felt for him, but somehow *enjoying* the illicit thrill of being with him.

She had told herself that, whatever her physical attraction, he just wasn't her type. Yet her disobedient eyes had strayed, and so had her mind. He was *exciting* and she had enjoyed the excitement. She had never felt anything like it in her life before, and that frightened her.

How could she feel like this for someone who was such an adversary? Where had her sense of judgement gone? Her brief, unhappy fling with Jefferson now felt indifferent and irrelevant. How on earth had she been upset enough to flee? And where had gone all those valuable lessons she had thought she'd learnt?

Panicked at thoughts piling up inside her, she feverishly concluded that her lack of experience had left her at the mercy of a man like Gabriel Ricci. She was also vulnerable after Jefferson, her bruised heart seeking affirmation that life carried on, whatever.

The power of his personality and the wild sexiness of his overpowering masculinity had wiped out all the caution she knew should have been in place.

Her heart was hammering and she was conscious of her nipples pushing against her T-shirt, unconstrained by a bra. Between her thighs, she could feel her arousal spreading.

'You…you don't know the first thing about me.' She breathed shakily, her blue eyes enormous. 'You think you do because I happen to come from a privileged background.' Her nostrils flared as she breathed him in. Was it her imagination, or had he closed the gap between them by a couple of inches?

'Why don't you tell me where I've gone wrong?' Gabriel murmured roughly, leaning down, his dark eyes scanning her face. 'I know that you're sexy as hell,' he growled. 'Rich, young and temptation on legs. All adds up to someone assuming that she can get exactly what she wants.'

Sexy as hell? Temptation on legs? He hadn't exactly given any indication that he might be thinking anything along those lines since she had entered his house.

Izzy felt giddy. She thought of him looking at her and thinking those things, and it was such an incredible turn-on that she had to bite down on a whimper rising up her throat.

'You think I'm *sexy*?' she heard herself ask, even as she realised that that was the very last thing she wanted to leave her lips. She was driven to look at him, and the hot flare in his eyes answered her question.

She licked her lips. They felt so dry. The breath stuck in her throat and she could hear her own shallow breathing. Her hands were pressed tightly behind her back.

And, in that moment, everything stood still as he lowered his head and kissed her.

Long, slow and easy—it was a kiss that was as heady as a drug, and the feel of his tongue against hers sent a wave of red-hot lust through her.

She freed her hands and linked her fingers behind his neck. She wanted him so badly…just for a minute. It was all wrong, of course it was, but…

Izzy closed her eyes and lost herself in that kiss.

CHAPTER FIVE

HE WAS THE first to pull away.

What the *hell*?

Gabriel raked his fingers through his hair, angry with himself, not so much for kissing her but for his lack of self-control. He hadn't meant to touch but he'd looked at her—looked at those sulky, full lips, the unruly chaos of her blonde hair and the narrowed brilliant cornflower blue of her eyes—and his body had just decided to do its own thing.

Never before had that happened to him. His supersonic rags-to-riches climb had driven out every single urge that could not be contained. In his life, there had been room only for ambition and he had willingly accepted that. Women were a pleasant distraction but never the main event. The main event had always been to reach such heady heights of power that he became untouchable.

It was what had brought Bianca to him. They had met at a wildly extravagant party held on a private island in the Caribbean. She had been there as

a friend of the family. He had been there because
the man who owned the island wanted to schmooze
him into doing a deal with one of his subsidiary
companies, a loss-making cargo airline business.
Gabriel had been there for exactly two days, just
long enough to get the information he wanted, but
not so long that he would actually have to circulate
with a bunch of people he was programmed to dis-
like. Rich, idle, beautiful.

Surrounded by barely clad young women, Bianca
had stood out because of her raven-haired, voluptuous beauty, and the fact that he could commu-
nicate with her in Italian had relieved some of his
boredom at being stuck on the island. It had amused
him to realise that he recognised her name, which
was synonymous with Italian royalty. It amused him
even further to think that the woman with the impeccable lineage hung onto his every word, pleased
as punch that she had managed to capture the interest of the one man there all the footloose and fancy-
free singletons wanted.

Obscenely rich, good-looking, ridiculously powerful. Worked wonders!

Had he been just another poor Italian guy trying
to eke out a living in the back streets of New York,
the story would have been quite different. He had
played with her on that island and then he had allowed himself to be coaxed into a relationship. She
had followed him back to Manhattan and, when she

had announced her pregnancy a handful of weeks later, there had been no option but marriage.

It had not been a cause for celebration but neither had it been a reason for despair. He hadn't figured on marriage yet, nor had he had any cravings to hear the pitter-patter of tiny feet, but with a *fait accompli* on his hands he had acknowledged that the security of his parents' relationship was something to aspire to rather than shun. They had always been there for one another and for him. Rather than succumb to the voice of doubt in his head, he had determined to make the best of the situation.

His parents had had massive reservations about Bianca and the wedding had been nothing short of a disaster, with her distinguished family members and rich, braying friends more or less side-lining his side of the family and his friends, all of whom he had invited in great numbers. Hell, he wasn't ashamed of his past, and people could take it or leave it as far as he was concerned.

But, given that dynamic, he should have predicted the fall of his marriage. He'd returned to his brutal work schedule, misreading—or perhaps, he'd thought afterwards, deliberately ignoring—the demands being made on his time with ever-increasing intensity. The drive to succeed was too ingrained to ignore.

Within weeks of Rosa being born, it had been evident that the union wasn't working, and really, it had just been a matter of time before a beautiful woman fine-tuned to expect male adoration found it in another man.

Gabriel had learnt many lessons from that experience, not least that he knew where he stood in the cutthroat world of making money, but when it came to women…? Well, in his world, trust in women was a commodity in very short supply.

Never again would he make the mistake of entering into any kind of relationship unless the rules of the game he was interested in playing were made crystal-clear. At all times, he would have complete control over his emotions.

As far as he was concerned, he'd tried longevity, and he wasn't cut out for it.

He had his daughter and that was all that mattered.

So now, here, to end up kissing some woman he'd known for five minutes *because he hadn't been able to help himself* struck him as a full-on admission of weakness.

The fact that this particular woman belonged to the same kind of world from which his dearly beloved ex came stuck in his craw even more.

'That shouldn't have happened,' he rasped, scowling. 'Accept my apologies.'

It infuriated him that his libido was still in full throttle, red-hot and pulsing as he watched her wipe the back of her hand across her mouth.

Her scowl matched his, and for a second he was wrong-footed by that reaction, because given the circumstances most women would have been trying to find a way towards a repeat performance.

She'd folded her arms and was now staring at him with open hostility. 'No, it damn well shouldn't!'

'In which case, why did you enjoy it so much?' he asked and was gratified by the slow burn of colour in her cheeks.

'I did not *enjoy* it! You took me by surprise.'

He'd taken himself by surprise too.

'It won't happen again. Look…' He shook his head, but he could still feel the urgent throb between his legs telling him that, whatever he happened to be saying, his body was contradicting every word. 'I'll be going to Chicago tomorrow. Staying overnight on business. Let's forget about what just happened and get back to square one.'

Izzy continued to glare.

Her whole body was on fire, as if a match had been struck. He'd kissed her and she'd gone up in flames like a heady teenager instead of a woman recovering from a broken affair. She should have pushed him away. She should have remembered that she was going to be careful when it came to involvement with the opposite sex. At the very least, she should have recalled just how much she disapproved of him and his tactics with the cottage.

Was she so stupid that she was going to allow him to charm her, the way he had charmed Evelyn?

When the much-maligned nanny Bella left the

sick bed and headed back to the call of duty, would Izzy cheerfully be dispatched, knowing that all she'd managed to achieve was to make his life easier by babysitting his daughter so that he could work, because he had charmed her into silence?

She was red-faced with mortification.

'I don't think that this arrangement is going to work,' she said with staccato jerkiness in her voice. She'd taken a few prudent steps back but those flames were taking their time dying down.

'Why not?'

'Because I… It would be uncomfortable…after this. It's not something that's going to just disappear because you say so…' After that kiss, how on earth would she be able to look at him without instant recall? How would she be able to fight the treacherous thought that one kiss wasn't enough?

'It would be only as uncomfortable as we allow it to be,' he said tersely. 'If you really don't think you'd be able to face me after this, then I can't stop you from leaving. But here's something to think about: maybe you wouldn't be able to face me for a completely different reason. Maybe you wouldn't be able to face me without wanting a repeat performance.' He looked at her in darkly brooding silence for a couple of tense seconds, then he brushed past her and began heading towards the commanding staircase that divided the sprawling mansion.

After a few seconds, Izzy sprinted behind him, heart hammering inside her. This was not how this conversation should end. This was not where this devastating kiss should take them, towards unresolved conclusions and angry exchanges. She reached out, tugged the sleeve of his shirt and he slowly turned around.

'It was just a kiss. You're right. Why should either of us feel uncomfortable?' She stumbled over her words and lowered her eyes. Standing on the step above, he absolutely towered over her, and she had to crane her neck just to meet his eyes.

He wasn't going to make this any easier for her, and she couldn't blame him, but he had said what he'd said, and she had to clear the air without her emotions getting the better of her and dictating her behaviour.

The silence lengthened. 'Things happen and...'

'And...?' he said softly, eyebrows raised, eyes still cool.

'I *don't* want a repeat performance, but even if I did,' Izzy admitted with grudging honesty, 'There's no way you should think that I would do anything about it. I...guess I overreacted because...' Her breath hitched in her throat and her voice tapered off into silence.

'You don't have to say anything more on the subject. You can keep the back story to yourself.' But when their eyes met she felt she could see curiosity in his. Or was that her imagination? The moment felt strangely intimate and for a few seconds she had the giddy sensation of standing on the threshold of something, although she had no idea where that sensation was coming from.

'I… When I came here, I was recovering from… Well, I was going out with a guy, Jefferson, who wasn't the person I thought he was.' She looked at him and smiled sheepishly. 'Sorry. You're not interested in a back story, and I don't know why I'm telling you any of this anyway. It's not your business. I just came after you because I don't want to leave either you or Rosa in the lurch, and I won't let what happened drive my behaviour. You took me by surprise, but I took myself by surprise even more, because I thought I was too hurt to respond the way I did…back there…to you…'

She began to turn away but paused when he said in a roughened undertone, 'I don't know about you, but I could do with a cup of coffee.'

No way… You've said what you wanted to say, now you can coolly and calmly go to bed, knowing you've set the record straight. There was no need for you to start babbling on about your private life because he isn't interested. He just feels a little sorry for you, and probably wants to make sure oil has been poured over every bit of troubled water. After all, he still wants you to look after his daughter…

'Okay.'

This time, he settled her into an oak-panelled sitting room that overlooked the pool at the back. Outside lights just about illuminated the still, dark water. The waving trees were dark shadows and the expanse of the vineyard was silent and orderly.

He reappeared with two cups of coffee, handed one to her and then pulled a chair over so that he was sitting right in front of her.

'You were saying?'

'I was babbling.'

'What happened?'

'It's all very boring,' Izzy mumbled. Why suddenly become coy? She'd invited this conversation by divulging details about herself he hadn't asked for. 'I came over to the States to take up a job setting up a hotel in Hawaii, and while I was there I stupidly got involved with a guy.'

'Why stupidly?'

'Please don't think that you have to be polite and listen to this,' she said, but she couldn't work out why she was willing to continue. Was it because something in those dark, dark eyes invited confidences? The same something that had made her talk far too much since she'd been here? Or was it because a part of her wanted to find out what a man made of the situation? It was okay to confide in your girlfriends, and Mia had been so sympathetic, but girlfriends took your side, and maybe she was curious to see what a man's response would be. Men, in her opinion, were always so…practical and prosaic, and this particular specimen took practical to the extreme.

She was so wet behind the ears. Had she dived

into something with Jefferson without judging the depth of the water first? Expected more than could be delivered? Of course she had.

But…and here was the thing…she wondered if maybe she had made some fundamental error of judgement that only a man would be able to spot.

She was uneasily aware that there might be another reason why she was sitting here.

She liked being in his company. He excited her and excitement could be addictive. Her lips were still burning from that kiss, and all of that gave an edge to being here with him that made her blood run hot.

'I never do anything out of politeness,' he said matter-of-factly. 'Tell me what happened. I'm interested.'

'I didn't know anyone when I came over here,' Izzy offered in a halting voice. 'I was fresh out of university and this was my first job.' Why tell him that it had been an arranged one? She already knew what he thought about her and her moneyed background. No need to remind him of it. 'I didn't know anyone. I made friends with this lovely girl, Mia, who took me under her wing and introduced me to all sorts of people. She's into surfing in a big way and that's where I met Jefferson.'

'Jefferson. … Let me guess…a fellow surfer? Content to trawl the beaches and avoid the responsibility of actually holding down a job? I could probably describe him as well. Tall and blond. Long hair, I'll bet, and an easygoing manner.'

'More or less,' Izzy admitted.

'I'm guessing he saw you coming a mile off.'

'What do you mean?'

'That type isn't confined to somewhere like Hawaii. Stick a pin on any map where's there's a beach crowd in a well-to-do area, and you'll find a Jefferson waiting to meet someone who can fund his lazy life choices. They're the ones who hold down casual jobs that just about cover the bills, but most of their time is spent eyeing up prospective donors willing to contribute to the cause of promoting their lifestyle.'

'He was fun,' Izzy said half-heartedly, cringing at the ease with which Gabriel had read the situation.

'I'm sure.'

'He made me feel free.'

'And explain how you were trapped before, Izzy.'

'I know you think that I'm a spoiled, privileged brat who's accustomed to getting her own way, but my life hasn't been as straightforward as you think.'

Her clear blue eyes defiantly dared him to challenge her, and accordingly he tilted his head to one side and looked at her in silence.

How could this man manage to get on her nerves, encourage her to open up *and* turn her on *all at the same time*?

'I don't have to explain myself to you.' She backed off from completely succumbing to whatever pull he had over her, tried to shake herself free of the spell he was weaving.

'Quite true.' He paused. 'Did the man eventually

ask you for money? You're right, you don't have to explain yourself to me, but I can tell from the expression on your face that I've hit the nail on the head. Trust me, you had a lucky escape.' He drained the remainder of his coffee and looked at her with brooding, veiled eyes.

Gabriel didn't do back stories and, as much as he was tempted to quiz her, he wasn't going to break habits of a lifetime. Doubtless, hers would be a tale of the poor little rich girl, lonely and misunderstood in her gilded cage.

He'd heard a number of similar tales over the years. Privileged backgrounds seemed to breed a disproportionate lot of angst in a certain type of woman.

He wasn't sure why he was so curious about this particular one but he wasn't going to explore the reasons. She'd slept with some man who ended up wanting to fleece her and she'd run away from whatever job she had because she couldn't deal with it. Experiences like that toughened up a person and it would toughen her up even though, right now, she looked immensely frail and vulnerable, with those delicately flushed cheeks and that hurt, defensive expression in her big, blue eyes.

He wondered whether that side of her was what his daughter found so appealing—the side that was strangely childlike, even though she could be as fierce and frankly more outspoken than most of the women he had surrounded himself with after his divorce.

He continued to look thoughtfully at Izzy, his thoughts cloaked by dark eyes that were adept at expressing as much or as little as he thought appropriate. Right now, he had no intention of expressing an iota of what was going through his head.

Izzy and Rosa had bonded and from that bond could come some very useful information. Slowly but surely, he was beginning to flesh out the bigger story of what life for his daughter was like with Bianca.

He had never wanted to play dirty, and had refrained from doing anything that conceivably could jeopardise his relationship with Rosa, but with the threat of having to fight to keep his daughter in the country the tides were beginning to turn.

If information could land in his lap without him having to do anything that involved Rosa feeling that she might be taking sides, then who was he to walk away from it?

And if that information could come via Izzy, with her clear, blue eyes and halting shyness, then why not encourage that conduit?

Solution-based as he was, Gabriel saw nothing wrong with his tactics. He would encourage confidences. Why not? He would see how things played out between them. Certainly that kiss advertised a chemistry that sparked, and so what if he used that chemistry to get to where he wanted to go? No hardship there. They were two adults. One thing might very well lead to another, and pillow talk could prove very rewarding.

He thought of that one thing leading to another and felt himself involuntarily harden in immediate and pleasurable response.

'I know that,' Izzy confided in a broken, halting voice. 'Not that it felt much like a lucky escape at the time.' No, it was devastating to realise that she had been wanted for what she had and not who she was.

'A broken heart,' Gabriel inserted, 'is never easy to deal with.'

'And you should know, I guess.' Izzy shot him a sympathetic look. 'Considering you're divorced. I'll bet you've suffered a lot more than I have.'

Gabriel stiffened, automatically primed to repulse any attempt by anyone to ask about his private life. He didn't deal in explanations and he had never met any woman who dared encroach beyond the No Trespass signs which were always glaringly in place.

But a bigger picture was taking shape, stamping over the ridiculous tightness in his chest at her story, and he knew that letting his guard down for once in his life would be a small price to pay.

He nodded curtly. 'Divorce is never pleasant,' he muttered.

'No, I can't imagine it is,' Izzy murmured. 'I'm sorry for you that it seems to have ended on such an acrimonious note, but I guess love and hate are just opposite sides of the same coin.'

Gabriel grunted.

'You don't want to talk about it.'

'Nothing to talk about,' he said and shifted, veiling his expression further. 'I prefer not to dwell on what's gone. Always more profitable living in the present and looking towards the future.'

'That's exactly what I came here to do,' Izzy admitted, sounding rueful.

'Until you became embroiled in the saga of the cottage and your mother's nanny...'

'Until that happened.' Izzy lowered her eyes and Gabriel could see the steady pulse in her neck, the gentle flush creeping into her cheeks. With some sixth sense he knew that she was torn between wanting to pursue a conversation about the cottage and not wanting to break the tremulous accord between them.

She looked up. For a split second their eyes met and held, and he smiled. There was a reason why she didn't want to ruin the electricity that had sprung up between them, and he had to concede that she wasn't on her own here. He was enjoying this sizzle of excitement, an undercurrent of tantalising, shimmering possibilities. That kiss had opened a Pandora's box and he, for one, had no intention of trying to shut it.

But neither was he going to make a play for her. He would let her come to him.

Was he using her? Maybe, but wouldn't she likewise be using him if they did what their bodies were clearly urging them to do?

She'd been hurt by some man she'd met on a

beach. Subconsciously, she wanted to be pieced back together. He could sense that from the little she had told him.

And, if he offered himself to be that helping hand for the job, then wouldn't he be doing her a favour?

Wasn't it, really, a mutually beneficial situation? Yes. It was.

'It's late,' he murmured, fluidly rising to his feet and waiting for her to follow suit, watching as she scrambled up. He moved closer to her whilst maintaining a respectable distance and murmured sincerely, 'And again, that kiss…not planned. It's not like me to…' He hesitated and then continued absolutely truthfully, 'To allow my attraction to any woman get the better of me. But on this occasion, I lost the battle. You were beyond temptation.'

He drew back and began heading towards the door, very much aware of her alongside him, so slender, seemingly so fragile and, oh, so tempting. He turned and gave her a mock-salute.

'I'm going to head to my office. I'll have time to say goodbye to Rosa before I leave for Chicago, and I'll see you when I get back day after tomorrow.' He paused and crossed another of his self-imposed boundaries. 'I'll let you have my personal line. You'll be able to get through to me any time you want.'

'We'll be fine.' Izzy smiled reassuringly.

'I know you will, and I can't wait to see you when I return.'

* * *

He called. Of course, Izzy should have known
that he would want to talk to her to find out how
Rosa was doing, but she was still flustered when
he phoned that first time, pretty much as soon as
he landed in Chicago. The dark timbre of his voice
sent shivers racing up and down her spine.

It brought to mind the devastating impact of his
kiss, the way his mouth on hers had made her feel.
It also brought to mind what he had said. He had put
his cards on the table, told her that he was attracted
to her and then he had walked away, leaving her
thoughts in a jumble.

He didn't pursue the conversation or make any
suggestive remarks when he spoke to her on the
phone. The fact that he was acting so *normal*, as
though nothing had been said between them, fuelled her fevered imagination like nothing else could
have done.

He was on her mind to an extraordinary degree,
even though she was as involved as always with
Rosa, taking her to pick fruit in Evelyn's garden
and drawing pictures of flowers, while Evelyn stu-
diously gave them both little lessons on their names
and origins.

She found herself waiting for his debrief call,
which duly came just before Rosa was to be settled
for the night. He chatted to her while Izzy faffed
and tried to subdue a rush of heady excitement and,
when he did ask to be put on the line with her, she

had to breathe deeply and count to ten before she could speak in a normal voice.

'Yes, everything's just great… We had a really busy day… Went to Evelyn's for tea… Rosa ate all her dinner… Oh, I'm sorry to hear that Bella is going to be in a bit longer than expected. Yes, see you tomorrow… Oh, you'll be back late? Never mind, have a safe trip…'

Afterwards, she replayed the conversation in her head and wondered whether there was anything to read between the lines. Had he completely forgotten about that kiss? About what he had said afterwards? He was a man of the world…maybe he was accustomed to that level of sophisticated, nonchalant flirting that didn't necessarily go anywhere. She'd reassured him that a repeat performance wouldn't be on the cards, so why was she so let down at the notion that he was simply doing as asked?

The more she thought about him telling her that he hadn't been able to resist that kiss, the more she burned with the forbidden desire to take things further between them.

It contravened all her resolutions never to get wrapped up with the wrong man again. Gabriel Ricci could not be *more wrong*. And yet…

The following day dragged. The skies were overcast but there was a dense humidity in the air that made both Rosa and her lethargic.

They had a light lunch and then, at a little after

five, when at last the humidity was dying down a bit, Izzy suggested the pool. They had yet to go swimming, partly because the swimming pool, spectacular though it was, had lost it novelty when compared to Evelyn's orchard and exploring her garden. Rosa had grown up with swimming pools and all the other accoutrements of extreme wealth. It was the simple stuff that intrigued her.

With Gabriel not due until well past the witching hour, they both got into their swimsuits, pulled out a few pool toys from the extravagant changing suite built under a canopy of trees by the side and splashed around for a while, playing silly games.

Rosa could swim like a fish. Izzy pretended she couldn't. They laughed and chatted, and it occurred to Izzy that she was discovering a whole lot about Rosa's life with her mother, things that made her wonder how on earth Gabriel could have fallen for the woman, who sounded monstrously selfish.

Post-divorce, he might admit that she was fond of playing games and used her daughter as a convenient pawn, but there must have been a time when he had been smitten, or else why would he have married her?

And yet she heard tales of Rosa being left to her own devices when there was no nanny around… of Rosa having to make herself scarce when her mother had her boyfriends over…of Rosa being removed from school without warning to go on inappropriate holidays or else being dumped with friends, awkwardly aware that at times she wasn't entirely wanted.

Most damaging of all, as far as Izzy was concerned, was the revelation that Bianca had warned her daughter to keep quiet about what happened on the home front *or else.* The pull to stay for the sake of Rosa, never mind Evelyn, was a powerful force in its own right.

In fairness, Rosa seemed blithely unperturbed, but surely, deep down, she was? Izzy knew from her own painful experiences just how fast and far a disjointed background could travel, screwing up your life for years to come.

The sky had darkened without Izzy noticing and it was only when there was the sharp crack of thunder overhead that she grabbed Rosa and began making a sprint for the house.

The heavens opened. Thunder rumbled, and the rain pelted down with such ferocity that by the time they hit the side door they were drenched.

She didn't have time do anything with her towel. She didn't have time to fling on her T-shirt. Nor did she have time to see anything in front of her because she was one hundred percent focused on both she and Rosa making it back through that side door into the kitchen without slipping on the suddenly treacherous paving.

So colliding slap, bang into an immovable object holding the kitchen door open was a shock, and she recoiled back in confused panic.

It took a few seconds of crazy blinking before she realised that the immovable object was Gabriel. He stepped back, hoisted Rosa off her feet and carried her into the kitchen and, voice high, Izzy couldn't help demanding what the heck he was doing there.

She was shivering with sudden cold, angry that he had surprised her, angry that she had been thinking about him non-stop, and angry that he clearly hadn't been thinking about her because there was not the remotest hint of *anything* when he slowly turned round to look at her.

He looked cool, collected and inscrutable as he glanced at her while whipping a towel from one of the drawers and clumsily wrapping it around Rosa, who had curled up against him like an insect burrowing for safety.

'Have you forgotten?' he asked wryly. 'This happens to be my house. I'm going to take Rosa up.' He paused, expression veiled. 'You should change, get out of those wet things. We can debrief later, once Rosa is settled.'

'I think I'll have an early night, if you don't mind.' Izzy knew that she was overreacting to the shock of seeing him when she hadn't expected to and to her own stupid thoughts about what he had said, what they had done and how quickly he had moved past it all while she had continued mentally to chew it all over like a dog with a bone. She was *piqued*. Pathetic.

'Of course.' He was already moving off, his pristine suit wet from Rosa dripping all over him. 'In that case, I'll see you in the morning.'

CHAPTER SIX

SHE COULDN'T SLEEP. What started as darkening skies, a rumble of thunder and a sudden downpour developed into a full-blown storm as the night wore on.

Izzy had closed all windows yet the force of the rain battering against them made her wonder whether the next sound she heard would be the shattering of glass.

Plus, she was starving.

She'd vanished up to her suite the evening before, head held high, smarting from the way she had allowed that man to climb into her head. That was all well and good but now, here she was, at a little after two in the morning, and the rumbling of her tummy was doing a great job of overpowering the sound of the rain pelting down.

Wide awake, she eased herself off her bed and wondered whether she should call Evelyn and find out if the older woman was okay. Was this sort of dramatic weather *a thing* in these parts of America? Would she be sleeping peacefully through the commotion because she was used to it? Would a phone call in the early hours of the morning to check she was okay have the opposite result, sending her into a state of blind panic?

In the end, she decided not to call. She would head down to the kitchen and get herself something to eat and something hot to drink. Why not? She was starving and she wasn't going to get back to sleep any time soon.

Despite the storm raging outside, it wasn't cold inside the house. She didn't possess a dressing gown and, rather than go to the bother of putting on jeans and a T-shirt for a midnight raid on the fridge, she crept downstairs in her pyjamas. Although her 'pyjamas' actually consisted of a pair of tiny shorts festooned with cartoon characters and a sleeveless vest which she had bought years ago from the boy's section of a department store in London.

She didn't bother with bedroom slippers and tiptoed like a thief in the night. The vast house was in complete darkness, and it took a little while for her eyes to adjust, but she was familiar with the layout now and working her way down to the kitchen wasn't a problem.

She imagined her mother doing this very thing when she'd been a kid but then she realised that the house would have been much smaller. The rush of nostalgia she had hoped to feel when she had embarked on this trip to Napa Valley hadn't materialised to the degree she had hoped and now, against all odds, she had come to associate this place with Gabriel and Rosa. Their story had eclipsed her mother's presence.

Their story ran the risk of eclipsing *everything*, including the very reason she was here, under this roof. Saving the cottage had taken a back seat as she had become involved with Rosa. What was Gabriel going to do? He never mentioned it, aside from that one and only time when he had informed her that the man Evelyn had spotted on the grounds had been hired a while back to inspect the outlying property.

Was he still thinking about whether to buy or not? To chuck Evelyn out on her ears with a pat on her back and a guilt-salvaging cheque with which to find herself somewhere else? Was he just conveniently using her to help with Rosa? Was stringing her along with vague promises that were never going materialise simply his way of getting her on board while he was nanny-less? He was ruthless, but how ruthless was he?

And had he actually meant it when he'd said that he found her attractive? Beyond temptation? Or had she simply been giving off some weird pheromones at the time which had prompted him to kiss her because he was a red-blooded male? Men, as it was well known, weren't fussy when it came to kissing women who wanted to be kissed.

All those thoughts were whirring round in her head as she peered into the fridge in search of food. She didn't hear a thing and she would have been

clueless if the lights hadn't been slammed on, causing her to jerk back, utterly losing her balance which
was unfortunate when she was holding a bottle of
milk in one hand and a jar of jam in the other.

Both were catapulted into the air and crashed to
the ground in a flurry of splintered glass, oozing red
jam and a spreading white lake of milk.

In the middle of the chaos, Izzy did her best to
struggle to her feet while holding on to the last ves-
tige of her dignity.

Gabriel.

Bare-chested and in a pair of pale-grey jogging
bottoms.

'What the hell?'

Izzy wanted to wail. Instead, she glared. She was
marooned in the middle of splintered glass, wet from
spilled milk and utterly mortified.

'Don't move, for God's sake.' He left the kitchen
at speed to return seconds later in a pair of loafers.

Izzy hadn't budged. She could scarcely breathe,
far less get her leaden limbs to work.

When she thought it couldn't get worse, it did, as
he stepped onto the glass and scooped her up in an
easy movement while she prayed for the ground to
open up and swallow her.

She looped her arms around his neck and was
instantly flooded with all those taboo thoughts that
had plagued her during the night.

The feel of him… The scent of him…

She stifled a moan, closed her eyes, aware of him

carrying her out of the kitchen, out into the hall and then up the winding staircase. But, instead of finding herself back in the relative safety of her bedroom when she next opened her eyes, she found that he had taken her to his suite.

Outside, the storm continued to rage. He had switched on a light by the bed and pools of shadow obscured the room. She could see enough to note just how relentlessly masculine it was. No excess furniture and everything concealed behind smooth, glossy, handle-less doors that banked one side of the wall. White on white with strips of walnut wood here and there. A wooden floor and a long floating shelf on which were three computers, two shut, one blinking. She could see an *en suite* bathroom through an open door. His room was roughly three times the size of hers, massive and minimalist.

'Don't stand,' he ordered, pre-empting her where she had been deposited by the window on a tan leather chair.

Izzy hugged herself. 'I want to go back to my bedroom.'

'I don't care what you want. I'm going to examine your legs in case you have any glass splinters anywhere.'

'I don't.'

'Bella is in hospital. Fancy joining her there with an infected leg because you're so damned stubborn?'

'I would know if I had a shard of glass sticking out of my thigh!' She feverishly followed him with her eyes as he disappeared into the bathroom and resurfaced with a black tin, squatting in front of her.

And then he began to examine her feet, very gently, feeling them, then her legs, his fingers smooth and cool against her skin, stirring her body into hot, shameful response.

Her heart was thundering and her mouth was dry.

'I was so quiet,' she whispered, fascinated by the sight of him kneeling in front of her.

'I have an alarm by my bed,' he murmured. 'It detects if anyone is moving in the house late at night and pin-points what room they're in.'

'You thought I was a burglar.'

'I live in an expensive house,' Gabriel murmured, still inspecting her, his voice low and soft as he worked his way up her thighs. 'Many have suggested I have bodyguards.'

'Oh.'

'I've never cared for the infringement that would bring to my personal freedom.' He glanced up at her and their eyes tangled for a couple of heart-stopping seconds. 'Besides, I'm skilled when it comes to fighting. Why did you go downstairs?'

'I was hungry,' Izzy whispered.

'You should have eaten something with me instead of running away upstairs.'

'I wasn't running away.'

'Weren't you?'

Her breathing hitched in her throat. 'I… I wasn't

expecting you earlier today...' she croaked. 'I thought you would be returning...later. You said...'

'I cut short a couple of meetings to return earlier.'

'Why? Rosa was perfectly fine here. I told you so when you called.'

Was he aware that he was still stroking her thigh, even though his dark eyes were fixed to her face with an intensity that made her all hot and bothered?

'Maybe my unscheduled arrival wasn't entirely about Rosa...'

'What do you mean?'

'You were on my mind.' He levered himself up and stood in front of her for a few seconds, towering, sending her thoughts into crazy meltdown.

The thrill of danger was like a feather trailing over her skin.

'I was?' she asked breathlessly.

'Does that surprise you?'

'You barely noticed me when Rosa and I ran out of the rain.' Stupid, *stupid*. Why on earth had she said that? Why had she let him glimpse that weakness in her?

Because he had said what he had... Because he had opened that door and invited her to walk through...

'Is that why you ran away? Did you want me to sweep you off your feet and carry you to my bedroom so that I could ravish you?'

'Of course not.' She felt her face flaming and her body was tingling, buzzing, as if she'd been plugged into a socket. He'd stooped back down so that he was at her eye level.

She wanted this man so much she was giddy with it. And the way he was looking at her… She half-closed her eyes and reached out and stroked the side of his face, and adrenaline rushed through her body in a tidal wave.

'No glass anywhere.' He lifted her up and she gave a startled yelp, but then her fingers were linking behind his neck, and she *wanted* this. 'But I should keep checking…just to make sure. And you're a little damp from that spilt milk. You should get out of those clothes, don't you think?'

'I should,' Izzy muttered against his chest.

He would be her first and, when she thought of giving her virginity to this man, every nerve in her body tingled with barely suppressed excitement.

She'd launched herself into a relationship with Jefferson and had thought, *expected*, that he would be *the one*. He'd been so attentive, so much fun, had taught her how to surf and teased her when she'd kept falling into the sea. And yet, much as she'd been attracted to him—because he *was* attractive, with that blond, blond hair—she hadn't felt like this, hadn't felt this helpless *yearning* that seemed so out of her control. She'd wanted to wait, had wanted to take a little time, get to know him properly.

Had part of her secretly suspected what had become obvious over time? That he wasn't the good-natured, thoughtful, carefree man she'd thought he was? Gabriel had teased so many confidences out of her without really trying, and yet to Jefferson she had been a closed book, skirting over the details of her life, maybe knowing that if she turned those pages too slowly he would soon become bored.

His tolerance had declined rapidly when she'd refused to sleep with him. At first, he'd been brilliant about it, but within a month she'd seen the sulky tightening of his mouth, and then the requests for cash had begun to creep in.

He was waiting for a cheque from his last job… could she lend him a couple of hundred for his rent? Of course he'd pay her back… And could he maybe have a few hundred more…? There was a surfboard he was desperate to get hold of…

And some underlying guilt that she hadn't jumped into bed with him had made her meet those demands, modest enough at first, until finally he'd produced a sketchy outline of a company he wanted to set up. A few boats…advertising costs…half a million would get things going and there'd be no looking back…

Izzy had fled, her pride in tatters, her ego far more bruised than her heart, although she was only now beginning to recognise that.

Thank God she hadn't jumped into bed with him. The thought of it made her feel sick. Yet, here she was, ready to jump into bed with a man who had made no attempts to butter her up with promises of a relationship. He was offering her sex, without even the benefit of some fancy wrapping, and the offer was irresistible and she just didn't get it.

She looked at him from under her lashes as he gently settled her on his bed and then drew back and looked at her.

'You sure about this?' he asked huskily.

Gabriel hadn't lied when he'd told her that she'd been on his mind. When he'd flown to Chicago, for the first time in his life the adrenaline rush of completing a deal that would add to his already staggering portfolio had failed to deliver its usual kick.

He hadn't been able to focus and it had driven him nuts. Since when had a woman come between him and his work? The answer to that was *never*.

Was it because this was not the normal progression when it came to his love life? Or was it because there was an ulterior motive underlying the situation? Had that given the routine boy-meets-girl, boy-beds-girl situation an added edge? Surely it couldn't be a simple case of wanting someone so badly you couldn't get them out of your head?

He had rejected that possibility and instead focused on the fact that from Izzy lay a direct path to his being able to exert some leverage over his rapacious and vindictive ex-wife.

He'd been keen to return to the vineyards, not just for Rosa, but because he was intensely practical, and if a plan had to put into action then the sooner things kicked off, the better. *That*, he concluded, had been the impetus behind his hurried return.

He had returned to a storm and as he had stood there at the door, ready to race outside, Izzy had come blindly running towards him, every scrap of her given over to protecting his daughter, making sure she was kept as safe as possible.

Something inside him had twisted. He didn't know what but it was a fleeting sensation of strange discomfort mixed with a melting warmth.

They'd been swimming and she'd been in an extremely modest black bikini that had still managed to do the utmost for her slender, gazelle-like body.

He'd taken Rosa, stepped back, temporarily blindsided by a rush of primal desire, and then…

Here she was. He couldn't think straight when his mind zoomed back to finding her in the kitchen… her peachy bottom sticking out as she'd peered into the fridge. Small pyjamas, without a hint of seductive *anything*, yet the most erotic get-up he had ever seen. Somehow he'd always gone for the woman in obvious designer gear but his tastes in women's fashion seemed to be drastically changing.

He wasn't sure what he would do if she had a change of mind but she smiled now, looked away then just as quickly looked back at him, her huge eyes oddly hesitant.

He smiled back, stepped out of his jogging bottoms and watched her mouth open with such blatant fascination that he was tickled pink.

Rich trust-fund babe she might be—and, God knew, all the sexual expertise that went with a life lived in the fast lane, whatever her appearances to the contrary—but, hell, wasn't there something just so damned *refreshing* about her?

Watching him watching her was the most sensual, erotic experience Izzy had ever had. She wriggled and, on cue, he joined her on the bed and she felt the brush of his erection against her thigh.

He was big, *really* big, and a shiver of nerves raced through her. But no way was she going to admit to being a virgin. He didn't think she was, and if he knew then he would run a mile. Something inside her told her that his casual invitation to have sex held an implicit assumption that they were on the same page when it came to coming together and then moving on, just a couple of ships passing in the night.

She trembled as he edged his fingers under her vest and gently began tugging it up until she felt the cool air on her breasts. Her eyes were closed and she was aware of his breath against her skin, warm and seductive.

Then he kissed her and she opened her eyes. This time the kiss was slow, sweet and leisurely and she arched up, yielding to it as their tongues meshed and his hands coiled into her hair.

Her breasts were pushed against his chest and her nipples were achingly sensitive as they grazed the dark hair on his torso. She was so wet, so turned on, too turned on to be nervous. But she knew that when that moment came she would have to grit her teeth not to reveal just how inexperienced she was.

'You're so beautiful,' he whispered into her ear and she smiled and wriggled.

'So are you.'

Gabriel burst out laughing and his dark eyes were amused when he drew back and looked at her for a few moments. 'That's very direct of you.' He smiled a slow, curling smile.

'I hate playing games.'

Gabriel didn't reply but he felt a twinge of guilt. He wanted information from her. Did that come with the label of playing games with her because he wanted to gain her confidence? No. If he hadn't been so damned attracted to her, then yes, but as it stood they were both doing what came naturally to them, and if he ended up where he wanted to be then that would be a fantastic additional bonus.

At the end of the day, he decided, no one was holding a gun to anyone's head and demanding state secrets.

'What are you thinking?' Izzy brushed his jaw and felt the roughness of stubble.

'I'm thinking that sex and chat don't go hand in hand,' he growled. With which he reached down, hooked one finger under her shorts and took them

off in one smooth movement, along with her underwear.

Silky-soft thighs, slender as a colt's. Her breasts
were small and pert, her nipples pink discs begging
to be licked.

Gabriel slowly moved down, trailing caresses
along her neck, tasting her skin, then he settled on
one of her breasts and sucked, drawing it into his
mouth while simultaneously nibbling her stiffened
nipple.

He looked at her. Her long, unruly hair was spread
in a blonde tangle across his pillow, her mouth was
parted, her nostrils flared and the tremble in her
body was a massive turn-on.

He continued to suckle at her breast, letting his
hand drift downwards over her flat stomach, feeling
as she sucked in a sharp breath. Then down lower,
over the jut of her hips and between her legs, going
nowhere in particular, just stroking, caressing and
ruffling her downy hair with the tips of his fingers.

Izzy could feel her whole body relaxing. What he
was doing…

She saw his dark head moving at her breast and
she moaned softly. She was barely aware of parting
her legs, inviting those teasing fingers to do more,
to find the spot that was throbbing, yearning to be
touched.

He moved down, and when he settled between
her legs she automatically stiffened, her first urge to

snap her legs together, because this was an intimacy too far. But even as she weakly tried, he placed his hands on her inner thighs, holding them apart, and then his tongue darted between the soft folds of her womanhood to find the swelling bud. Over and over he teased it until she went mad, until she could hold off no longer and she came explosively against his questing tongue.

That complete abandon shocked her and she lay still, slowly coming down from her high, but then feeling her senses begin to respond even as he remained where he was, gently blowing on her, then kissing away the last of the shudders that had racked her body.

She groaned, lifted her legs a little, shivered and looked down at him buried between her thighs. The urge to tell him that she was a virgin was strong, but stronger still was the urgent need for him to continue, not to pull away in disappointment or shock.

The burden of her inexperience struck her. How should she pleasure him? If she touched him, surely he would see her awkwardness?

She tentatively wriggled away from caresses that threatened to spike to another orgasm. She wanted him in her, dreaded it yet yearned for it. She didn't want to reach another climax against his mouth. Never had her virginity felt more of an albatross round her neck.

She knelt and inched closer to him. With her free hand, she reached to feel the weight of him and felt a heady rush of delight when he groaned in instant response. As she took him between her hands and did what felt natural, and when he covered her hand with his own, guiding her to a steady rhythm, she fell into a groove, breathing fast, melting inside as her body heated up at the feel of him.

She kissed his chest, nibbled a flat, brown nipple and grew hotter and wetter.

Gabriel could barely hang on to his self-control. He was always the one in charge. He called the shots when it came to love-making but now, for the first time, someone else was taking him to places that were new and unexplored.

The gentle teasing of her mouth on his chest, on his nipples, was exquisite. The softness of her touch on his throbbing penis was driving him insane. The turn-on of her shy caress was overpowering.

He clasped the back of her neck, fingers tangling in her hair, and drew her back so that he could kiss her.

'I…have…never…' he confessed brokenly, barely recognising his voice, 'Wanted any woman as much as I…want you now…'

His kiss drove her back against the pillows and he continued to kiss her even as his hand blindly sought her wetness, delving to feel it slippery against his fingers.

He broke off to don protection, which took a matter of seconds yet seemed to drag as long as a lifetime, and as the cool air settled on her Izzy felt a rush of nervous panic.

She flinched back just a fraction as he settled over her, his big, powerful body a vision of strength and muscle. He nudged her entrance and she held her breath, waiting for his entry, praying it wouldn't hurt.

'Be gentle,' she gasped as he pushed deeper. She wanted so much to grit her teeth and find a way through her nerves and the pain she expected, and she was now realising that it had been naïve to assume that a man of his experience would be fooled.

She cried out as he plunged in deeply. The pain was sharp and her eyes were closed, squeezed tightly as he stilled, looking at her. She could sense the glint of his questioning eyes on her face and she refused to meet those questions head-on.

'Izzy,' he moaned huskily.

'Please don't stop,' she whispered.

'I must.'

'No!' Her eyes flew open and she looked at him fiercely. Both her hands reached to cover his taut buttocks, urging him on.

'You should have told me.'

'Please stop talking,' Izzy all but begged. 'I want this. I want *you*.'

She shifted, her body as supple as an eel's, encouraging him to keep going, not to leave her like this, awash with frustration and disappointment.

It seemed vitally important that this beautiful,

ruthless and utterly inappropriate man hold her hand and take her through the door that had been opened.

She pulled his head down, arched up and kissed him while he was still inside her and, when he groaned and began to move, she knew that he couldn't *not*.

The nerves had dissipated. The burst of pain she had felt had subsided to a dull, throbbing ache but that was eclipsed by something else as he skilfully moved in her,

How could he do that? How could he angle his body *just so*? How could he make her forget that this was her first time?

He filled her, taking it slow then moving faster, slow and easy one minute, ever deeper the next, until he had developed a tempo that began carrying her away.

He found the spot inside her with expert accuracy and as he pushed against it, over and over, a sensation of soaring began to rise inside her and she succumbed to it, loving the pleasure he was giving her and the pleasure she knew she was giving him.

Her orgasm was shattering, unexpected in its intensity and coming in waves. Izzy heard herself sob a wrenching response just as he arched back, stiffened and had one final plunge that took him over the edge.

He collapsed onto her, but only for a few seconds, then he shifted immediately to move onto his side.

He propped himself up on one elbow, and she said without looking at him, 'I don't want to talk about it.'

'That's not an option, I'm afraid.'

'I'm sorry.' Izzy could feel her eyes beginning to well up. Could there be a more crushing anti-climax to what had been the most wonderful experience of her entire life?

'Jesus, Izzy. Look at me.'

She glared at him. 'Why does it matter whether I was a virgin or not?'

'Because if I'd known,' Gabriel grated, 'I wouldn't have…made love to you.'

'Why not? You didn't force me into doing anything!'

'That's not the point, *tesoro*.'

'Then what is?'

'You don't know me, Izzy. I'm…' He sifted his fingers through his tousled hair and met her eyes steadily, seriously. 'I'm not capable of committing to any kind of relationship with you. You've been hurt by some bastard in all sorts of ways and you're inexperienced… You're probably searching for a replacement, someone to fill whatever void has been left inside you by some loser you're better off without.'

Gabriel couldn't remember ever having dug so deep into someone's motivations and psyche. Even as his marriage had been falling apart, he had guiltily acknowledged that he should have asked far more questions, expressed more curiosity, verbalised more. Instead, he had weathered the defensive aggression of his soon-to-be ex, seeking only to get on top of the practical issues.

A virgin! He couldn't credit it, but then he thought of the way she blushed despite her stubbornness and her fighting spirit. He had written off that crazy notion as existing only in his mind because the facts spoke for themselves. She was young, beautiful and rich and those attributes lent themselves to a pattern.

He'd been wrong.

Where he had before justified to himself how their mutual attraction could play into his hands, because all was fair in love and war, he was now assailed with a barrage of misgivings.

They had made love, and there was nothing he could do about that, but his conscience was telling him that he should get out now. Get out because she was vulnerable. Trust-fund babe she very well might be, but the usual attributes appeared to have passed her by.

'Don't you *dare* try to analyse me,' Izzy hissed. Her voice wobbled. 'You don't know what I'm thinking. You don't know what's going through my head.'

'Izzy…'

'Don't you *dare* "Izzy" me.'

'I don't want to be responsible for hurting you,' Gabriel confessed in a roughened undertone.

'What makes you think you could ever hurt me?' she asked. He didn't want soft and fluffy and he didn't want the girl with the broken heart. It wasn't what he was used to and, if nothing else, pride now stiffened her backbone. No way was she going to allow him to feel sorry for her. She'd spent weeks feeling sorry for herself. She didn't need someone else adding to the pity tally.

'Explain.'

'You're not my type,' she told him bluntly, and when he half-smiled she glared. 'You have such an oversized ego, Gabriel Ricci! You're attractive but that still doesn't mean that you're my type.' He lowered his eyes, sheathing his expression, but she was pretty sure that the wretched man didn't believe a word she was saying and her pride stiffened just a little bit more.

'I'm not drawn to business men. I like men who are a little more relaxed when it comes to living life. Jefferson turned out to be a creep, but that's life. You're a good-looking guy, Gabriel, and I suppose you know it, but there's a big difference between being physically attracted to someone and seeing them as relationship material. You're not relationship material, and I would have guessed that without you having to tell me.' She paused, looking at him steadily, while her rebellious mind busied itself with stupid, pointless thoughts.

What would it be like to have the heart of this dangerous, sexy, impossible man? Was he so cold, so ruthless, so driven because he had never stopped loving an ex-wife who now made his life hell, from the sounds of it? Had that been his one big love? Had that first cut been the deepest?

'We made love because I wanted it as well,' she said. 'And I thought it was great. I'm not interested in a relationship with you and I wish you had just… let things be, Gabriel. One night of pure pleasure without the drama afterwards.' She clenched her jaw until it ached. 'Instead, you had to make a big deal of it. Okay, so you think it was a mistake. Fine.'

She began to shuffle off the bed, taking the sheet with her. 'I'll be on my way. I'm sorry about Rosa, I know she'll be disappointed, but I don't think I can hang around here trying to make sure I get out of your way because you're turned off by me.' She could have added that Rosa, already the innocent victim of so much instability in her life, hardly needed more thrust upon her. To leave sooner would be a million times better for his daughter than if she were to leave later.

She wanted so much to try and persuade him to just stop pressuring Evelyn to sell up. She had seen this as an opportunity to wear down his inexorable need to own more at the expense of someone else. But she hadn't been able to withstand the chemistry between them and now everything was ruined. He would surely proceed with his plans. He couldn't chuck Evelyn out but he could simply wear her down until she acquiesced. Weren't there many ways to skin a cat, after all? He'd wanted someone else, not her. He'd seen the packaging and liked what he saw, but what was inside the wrapping paper wasn't what he thought he'd ordered, and now it was time to return to sender.

The sting of hurt was overwhelming. She chewed her lip and ungracefully continued to shuffle away, but she felt the clamp of his hand on her arm and she froze immediately.

'What the hell, Izzy? You think I *don't* fancy you?'

'I think I'm not what you signed up for. Which is the same thing, as far as I'm concerned.'

She tried to tug away from him but he drew her back against him and held her close, arms around her, even though she did her best to pummel her way free.

'You've given me the most precious gift any woman could give a man.' He spoke gruffly, his mouth buried against her neck, her hair falling across him soft and silky. 'I am not worthy of it. I may have got my words wrong, but don't think for an instant that what we just shared wasn't as amazing for me as it was for you.'

'You don't have to lie to spare my feelings,' Izzy whispered.

'Lie? Feel me, *amore*, touch me, and you'll find out fast enough just how much I fancy you…'

The fight drained out of her. Sitting here, breathing him in, he filled her. She recognised her weakness and accepted it.

CHAPTER SEVEN

GABRIEL LOOKED AT his daughter and Izzy, heads to-gether, one white-blonde, the other raven-dark.

They were counting fish, which wasn't difficult, because the three of them had managed to catch the grand total of two fish over a period of several hours. They were at a trout farm, owned and run by the same family for a million years. Their poles and bait had been provided and they had been taken to the beautiful, well-stocked pond and left to do their thing. When they were ready, the fish would be cleaned by one of the owners and they would grill it on site and eat it with the massive picnic that had been prepared by his housekeeper.

With Rosa in tow, Gabriel's activities had led him to places hitherto unexplored. The sanitised early-evening meals out in expensive New York restau-rants—with the occasional trip to the zoo thrown in when he took a break from work, which had been rare—were gone. In their place was a selection of fun activities meticulously researched by Izzy and enthusiastically seconded by Rosa.

He had not been allowed to renege on any of these activities because, Izzy had said four days earlier, Bella would be back soon enough and their routine would settle into place, so why not take advantage of the window of opportunity?

Bella would be returning over his dead body.

He continued to look thoughtfully at the pair of them, utterly absorbed in what they were doing, as close as conspirators plotting.

He hadn't asked Izzy anything. Hadn't engineered the conversation in any direction. He had backed off because they were lovers now and, while she certainly played it cool, made it clear that she wasn't in it for anything long term, he was still uneasy with the notion of outright exploiting their situation.

For once, his motto 'the end justifies the means' didn't seem entirely appropriate. A conscience he'd been unaware of had made itself felt.

That said, she had talked, soft, lazy and drowsy when good sex had blurred the edges and lowered any qualms she might have had when it came to confiding. In between the titbits about how she and Rosa spent their time when he was working—the home baking, the den making and the paper-boat racing—he had learnt some rather interesting facts about his daughter's life when he wasn't around.

Bianca seemingly was around far less than she

made out. There were lots of trips abroad. He had already got one of his people to tabulate just when those trips had occurred, for how long and with whom?

School was an institution randomly adhered to, with Rosa being removed for things as trivial as manicures and pedicures. What six-year-old needs a manicure? He had barely been able to contain his fury. As with the trips abroad, he had compiled a dossier on all those pointless visits.

No wonder Bella had settled into home schooling. Rosa would need it, judging from her sketchy class attendance.

There had also been men back at the house and, whilst Gabriel did not expect his ex-wife to be a paragon of celibate virtue, he wondered at just how cavalier she was when it came to inviting them back. This last item he had found out from Rosa, who had casually chatted about some man having lunch there.

It had taken every iota of willpower not to get on the phone and lay all his information at his dear ex-wife's door. However, he would play a waiting game. He would garner his facts and he would plan his manoeuvres. There was nothing to be gained from undue haste.

And, in the meantime, his conscience was clear. On every front, he had played it fair and square. He hadn't prised information from Izzy, hadn't asked questions and had been upfront so that, when the time came for them to bid farewell, it would be done without room for accusations about promises made but not delivered.

On the subject of the cottage? The topic had been raised in a roundabout manner just the once and he had skilfully diverted the conversation because, really, business was business. Maybe he would take her on a sightseeing tour of some of the more desirable places in the valley, open her eyes to where life could be perfectly liveable for a woman in her late seventies.

Right now, though…

On so many levels, things were going much better than he could ever have anticipated. He began moving towards them. One week, he decided, and he would have to move on. He would start the ball rolling by telling Bianca that Bella's services would no longer be required and should she throw a hissy fit… Well, this time round she might find that she couldn't hold a man to ransom when he'd stockpiled sufficient ammunition.

Izzy discovered that she was becoming adept at putting off thinking about when the end of this strange relationship with Gabriel was going to come.

She had agreed to be Bella's replacement in good faith. She had seen it as a way of inserting herself into his routine, finding opportunities to persuade him that he must not buy the land to increase his holdings, must not pull the house out from under Evelyn's feet. On site, she'd reasoned, she would be able to work away at him, dismantle his plans bit by bit, or at least *try*.

But they had become lovers a week ago and since then she had broached the subject of the cottage once, and he had had nothing to say on the subject. He had shrugged, told her something vague about tallying up the costs of ditching the project, waffled on for a couple of minutes about the difficulties of stopping the tide once the barriers have been raised and then promptly changed the subject.

And she had let him because she had fallen under his spell. The minutes, the hours, the days… She was drifting on a cloud and she didn't want to spoil things by bringing reality into the equation.

She'd thought that he would continue to devote his time to his work but she had been surprised at the alacrity with which he'd conceded when she had sternly told him that he needed to come with her and Rosa to all the stuff she'd lined up.

Bella would be back soon enough, she'd said, and he'd looked at her without saying anything for a while, then lowered those fabulous eyes of his and agreed.

Since then, they'd been to a medieval-themed castle winery that had all the atmosphere of a sorcerer's castle with its moat and drawbridge and towers and ramparts, and a torture chamber that Rosa had adored. They'd been ice-skating at a rink which was open all year round, and they'd been apple-picking

and sampled home-made ice-cream from a legend-
ary ice-cream shop in Sebastopol.

Everything in this part of the world felt lazy, and
the vastness of the scenery helped her feel as though
she was living in an alien landscape, in a sort of
dream world.

It disturbed her that she didn't want any of it to
end.

She gazed up at the house from where she was
standing by the pool. It was a little after ten-thirty
and for the first time they had been out to dinner,
having Evelyn over for Rosa for the evening.

Izzy was still in her finery. Gabriel had nipped
upstairs to check on Rosa, having delivered Evelyn
back to her cottage.

'Let's have a nightcap by the pool,' he'd suggested. 'Rosa will be safely asleep, and we could
even have a swim. There's nothing more invigorat-
ing than having a swim at the end of a muggy day.'

Izzy strolled to one of the chairs by the side of
the pool, sat down and drew her knees up to clasp
her arms around them. When she tried to chart the
progression of her feelings for Gabriel, she got lost
along the way. How could her seething antipathy
have turned into something that held her fiercely
captive? How could *lust* have morphed into real feeling? Izzy didn't want to put a name to what that
feeling was, but it hovered on the periphery like a
flash of something caught out of the corner of the
eye, gone before the brain had time to register it.

She found him exciting. Arrogant, infuriating but *exciting*. Even before she'd taken the job of helping with Rosa, even when she'd been gritting her teeth and wanting to *hit* him for the anxiety he was causing Evelyn, there had still been something about him that had begun to suck her in, something intense that made the hairs on the back of her neck stand on end.

She disapproved of him, yet she was drawn to him like a moth to a flame.

He wasn't her type, yet her body curved to his like a flower bending to bask in the warmth of the sun.

Nothing about what she felt made sense yet even now, sitting here, thinking logically about what was happening in her life, she still couldn't control the shimmer and sizzle of anticipation when she thought of him joining her out here and then, later, lying in bed with her, taking her.

She heard the soft pad of his feet and smiled, her body already heating up, as though she'd suddenly been plugged into a socket and the switch turned on.

'Penny for them…'

'I was just thinking what a lovely meal that was.' Izzy would never tell him what was going through her head. Far safer to stick to the uncontentious. 'Made a change going out.'

'It did.' He paused, swerving round to tug her to her feet and gather her in his arms. He didn't kiss her immediately, though, just gazed down, their eyes meeting as he brushed a strand of blonde hair from her face.

She'd dressed up for the evening. Had actually had to go out and buy something.

'I like the dress, by the way,' he murmured, hands on the small of her back gently nudging her against him. 'Thin straps, long zipper down the back… It's a dress made to be removed without too much fuss.'

He was in a pair of black trousers and a white shirt and he'd cuffed the sleeves to the elbows.

He couldn't have looked sexier.

She wound her arms round his neck and drew her to him, reaching up to kiss him, luxuriating in the mesh of their tongues and the pulse of his hardness against the flimsy silk of the dress.

'Swim?'

'Can't be bothered to go and get my swimsuit,' Izzy confessed.

'Who's talking about swimsuits?' He grinned, drew back and tugged down the straps of the dress, unzipping the zipper with seamless ease.

'Gabriel, *no!*'

'Why not?'

'Because…'

'There's no one here to see,' he murmured, cupping one small breast and rubbing the pad of his thumb over her nipple. 'These grounds are completely private, and the access gate to the back here is locked. Rosa is fast asleep. There's just the two of us…and I want you so much. I wanted you through that entire tasting menu. Thought it was never going to end.'

Izzy laughed softly. The dress had caught at the waist. She began undoing the buttons of his shirt but then her patience ran out and she tugged it free of the waistband and pushed her hands underneath to feel his flat nipples and the sprinkling of dark hair on his chest.

He tore off the shirt, ripping the bottom two buttons in his haste, and she followed suit with the dress.

Bit by bit, they somehow managed to get rid of their clothing while making unsteady progress towards the back of the sprawling patio with its trellised roof zig-zagged with tumbling flowers.

The wooden outdoor furniture was low, sleek and comfortable, made for stretching out on and relaxing under the shade on a balmy Californian day, the glorious infinity pool within sight.

At this time in the evening, poolside lights just illuminated the pool. The water was still and silvery, reflecting the light from the almost-full moon. The sky was velvet black and dotted with stars and the air was beautifully warm. Izzy could almost hear the soft rustle of the vines stretching for acres all around them. The silence was broken only by their breathing as they settled onto one of the long outdoor sofas.

He manoeuvred her so that she was half-lying, half-sitting, her feet on the ground, legs bent at the knees, and he sat between them and gently blew on the darker blonde curls there.

Izzy sighed and squirmed into a less awkward position, her whole body eagerly waiting for him to slide his tongue between the folds of her womanhood, to find the bud of her core and tease it until she was hurtling towards an orgasm.

He knew just when to draw back, when to switch his caress to the soft skin of her inner thigh, giving her time to slowly ease away from an orgasm, to climb down from her fevered high.

His dark hair was springy between her fingers. In her mind, the contours of his beautiful face were as familiar to her as her own. She could have traced his body blindfolded and knew that that body was his.

She grunted as he wound his way up along her naked body to settle his mouth on her nipple, swirling his tongue over it until she was going mad with wanting more.

'Protection,' Gabriel groaned. 'Where is it when you need it? We're going to have to have some fun without it…'

They did. She took him between her hands, into her mouth, held the weight of him as she slowly, rhythmically stroked him until he had to pull her away to give himself time to find some self-control and then, in the end, he couldn't hold off and he spilled over.

He explored every inch of her burning body with his mouth, his tongue and his fingers, teasing and tormenting until she gave a spasm against his fingers, writhing and arching back, missing the deep thrust of penetration but relishing the waves of pleasure his mouth and fingers could give her.

Afterwards they continued to lie on the sofa for a while, chatting, still naked, their bodies shimmering under the moonlight.

The moment felt fragile and Izzy wanted to hold it tight for ever. In an instant, it would be gone and they would part ways. She felt her stomach tighten and there was a sick giddiness inside her when she thought about them walking away in separate directions.

She wanted to cling but couldn't.

Had she done the unthinkable? Had she fallen for this inappropriate stranger? Her skin felt clammy. *This* was the feeling that had been hovering on the edge of her mind, as wispy as a tendril of smoke curling in the sky from a conflagration below, and just as dangerous.

'When is Bella due to return?' She broke the silence and began shifting to get to her feet, suddenly restless at the disturbing thoughts swirling through her head.

The air suddenly felt cool. She was retrieving her dropped garments when he stood and caught her from behind, hands at her waist, tugging her back against him so that she was pressed with her back to his stomach. Skin against skin, their bodies were still hot and damp from making love.

'What about that swim?'

'I'm not sure I'm in the mood,' Izzy said, heart beating fast and hard inside her as a series of conclusions formed in her head.

Love? How could she have fallen in love with this man? Hadn't she told herself that it was just mutual attraction? How could her body have disobeyed her head?

'It's really late.' She hesitated, suddenly anxious to have some idea as to where this was all going. It was one thing to be philosophical about enjoying what she had and living in the moment but it was quite another putting those noble ideas into practice.

Right now, all she could think of was a place in the very near future that inevitably would be painful.

'And you still haven't mentioned Bella,' she reminded him casually, prising away from his clasp and, without looking at him, flinging the dress over her and sticking on her underwear.

He slung on his trousers as she began walking away and stumbled a bit behind her before catching her by the arm.

'What's wrong?'

'Nothing.'

'Really?'

'You don't know me as well as you think you do,' Izzy said with an edge in her voice. 'Nothing's wrong. I'm just…tired, that's all. I don't want to have a midnight swim. Is that a crime?'

'She won't be.'

'Sorry?' Izzy turned around reluctantly. She didn't want to look at him. The minute she clapped eyes on him, all her willpower evaporated, and right now she didn't want evaporating willpower. If she had to get her act together, then she would have to start thinking about getting it together now. There was no point pretending to herself that she could handle the situation and take what was on offer while the offer was there.

'Bella. She won't be returning.'

'Why not?'

'Don't look so shocked.' Gabriel grinned, took her hand and began leading the way back to the house.

'Is…is she okay? I mean, I should probably have shown more concern but…'

'Oh, she's fine. In fact, due to leave hospital to-morrow.'

'Then, why—?'

'I sacked her.'

'You *sacked* her? But I thought… I thought that… isn't she related to your ex-wife?'

Gabriel shrugged. 'That doesn't confer lifelong immunity to being sacked.' His voice was flat and hard. 'When I see you with Rosa, I realise just how far Bella fell short of the ideal.'

He'd *sacked* Bella! Suddenly, the threat of what they had ending didn't feel quite so imminent. Cravenly, she realised that a respite would give her a bit more time to think.

'So, have you…found a replacement?' She watched as he pushed open the patio doors that led to a huge utility room beyond the kitchen. It sparkled in a way very few utility rooms did. This particular one, done up to the very highest standard, housed appliances that were all hidden away behind glossy grey doors. Even the shoes, boots and other paraphernalia of outdoor use had their own special cupboard which was tidied daily by a member of staff.

Izzy hovered and finally allowed her eyes to settle on him.

He looked tousled, his dark hair every which way. He hadn't bothered with the shirt, which he had obviously left dumped on the ground where they had been, and the top button of his trousers was undone. He was barefoot. The black loafers were doubtless with the shirt and both would be dutifully tidied away the following day by the same smiling girl who kept the utility room shiny and spotless.

She knew she looked as rumpled as he did. Her hair was a tangle down her back and she was likewise barefoot, although she had her shoes in one hand.

'It's not something that can be rushed,' Gabriel murmured.

'She must be upset to have been told that she would no longer be required, especially as she's still recovering from surgery.'

'I offered her a year's worth of pay. Whatever

feelings of despondency she might have had were thankfully short-lived.'

They were moving out of the utility room, opening the door to the kitchen. The house was more or less in darkness. Upstairs, lights on the wide landing were on, but down here they emerged into a pitch-black kitchen.

They didn't see the figure opening the kitchen door just as they were exiting the adjoining utility room.

Izzy was far too busy projecting all manner of unlikely possibilities that might be attached to his pronouncement. *Was this a way of ensuring that she stuck around for a bit longer? He hadn't said a word about a future between them, but if there was no replacement nanny on the scene then didn't that imply that he was happy for things to carry on as they were? And, if that was the case, then could there be the slimmest chance that, like her, he had become more involved in their relationship than he had anticipated—even if that might be something he would not want to admit?*

Looking down at Izzy's bent head, Gabriel was wondering what she was thinking. She gone into a funk earlier and he had no idea why. He didn't do women in a funk but this time it had jarred. He'd wanted to find out why.

Had the Bella situation been playing on her mind? It was the first time she'd mentioned the other woman. Was she uneasy about the prospect of an indeterminate stay at the house? Typically, he had taken it as a given that she would have no objection to sticking around for as long as he wanted her to, but now it occurred to him that he might have misjudged the situation. How, he wondered, would he react if she told him that she was on her way out?

When Gabriel considered that option, it surprised him just how unwelcome her departure would be. Surely he was no longer reliant on her for any information she might be able to pass on? When he had telephoned Bianca three days previously to tell her that Bella's services would no longer be required, he had coldly put her straight the second she had begun to launch a counter attack.

'Accept it,' he had informed his ex-wife, 'Or I'll play hard ball and you won't like it.'

And, when she had begun to go down the usual route of reminding him of all his shortcomings as a parent, he had softly imparted a few words of wisdom of his own and she had shut up. For the first time since the divorce, he had the weaponry with which to fight her and he intended to make full use of it.

Both preoccupied, Izzy and Gabriel only woke to the realisation that someone was in the kitchen when the lights were switched on, flooding the massive space with blinding fluorescent light.

And there she was.

* * *

Gabriel had said very little about his ex-wife, aside from her skill at manipulating the custody order. For a man as proud, as ruthless and as sharp as Gabriel, Izzy had seen it as a testament to his bone-deep integrity that he had refrained from setting the dogs loose on her to get what he wanted with his daughter. He had stepped back to avoid Rosa unwittingly being dragged into a row that wasn't her concern and that had been admirable.

Personally, she didn't think the woman had a leg to stand on, given everything Rosa had let slip over the time they had spent together.

At any rate, he hadn't described what Bianca looked like, but straight away Izzy knew that this was his ex. Five-foot-nine of sizzling, raven-haired, voluptuous beauty stood in the doorway of the kitchen with an expression that could have slain Medusa.

Izzy automatically took a step back, using Gabriel as a shield.

'Bianca,' he said, gathering himself with what Izzy considered formidable self-control. 'What the hell are you doing here?' His voice was glacial and Izzy shivered.

Bianca, on the other hand, looked far from cowed. She took a couple of aggressive steps towards him. Her black eyes were positively spitting fury.

'What do you think, Gabriel? You tell me that you're sacking my nanny and you expect me to nod and agree without a fight? I flew straight back and rushed here to demand an explanation!'

She moved with panther-like grace to look at Izzy through narrowed eyes and this time her expression was one of triumph. 'And I see that nothing has changed with you, Gabriel.' She folded her arms and continued to stare at Izzy. 'I hope you're not getting any ideas, my dear,' she said. 'But, if you are, I should point out that my darling ex-husband is only interested in short-term prospects.'

She turned to Gabriel while Izzy tentatively eyed the kitchen door and toyed with the idea of making a run for it. 'This one is a change for you, isn't she? Nondescript little creature. And bringing her back here? With my daughter sleeping upstairs? Not such a good idea, Gabriel.' She wagged her finger. Izzy held on to her temper through gritted teeth. This wasn't her fight and she wasn't going to get involved, whatever the bait thrown at her.

She thought that this might be what it felt like to be trapped on a battlefield with opposing sides firing cannonballs overhead.

'You think you can threaten me while you continue to womanise with every cheap floozy who happens to take your fancy? I don't think so!'

Finally, Gabriel moved and there was something menacing in his lack of urgency. A simple half-turn towards Izzy, a couple of steps towards her, and then he rested his arm across her shoulders.

What the heck was going on here?

Izzy was mesmerised by Bianca, so beautiful, so larger than life, so flamboyantly exotic, so unashamedly *furious*. A hissing, spitting cobra with deadly venom. She barely noticed the very slight squeeze Gabriel applied to her shoulder.

'You're a disgrace, Gabriel!'

'And you, Bianca, are not welcome in this house. I should have made sure to get the key from you a long time ago, but as I didn't I'll rectify the oversight now.' He held out his hand. Incredibly, it was as steady as a rock. Had the man *no* nerves at all? Izzy thought.

Izzy saw the flash of doubt replace the fury and the triumph on the other woman's face.

'I deserve to have a key so that I can check and see just what is going on behind my back. My daughter is my primary concern. I *knew* that coming here, *surprising you*, would be a good idea. I could have waited until morning, but no, I *knew* from the very second you decided to sack Bella without running it by me that you were up to something. I *knew* that if I showed up here at night I would catch you redhanded. You disgust me, Gabriel Ricci. Well, I can only say that my lawyer will be *very* interested to hear about what goes on when the lights are off and my daughter is asleep and you are in charge.'

'Bring it on, Bianca,' Gabriel said with silky softness. 'My fiancée and I would love nothing better than to rectify whatever misguided impressions you may care to divulge.'

'Fiancée? *Fiancée*, Gabriel?' But there was a sudden ashen pallor beneath the rich, olive skin.

'You know where the door is. Leave. And just remember, Bianca…you have been warned.'

CHAPTER EIGHT

THE KEY WAS flung on the ground. Gabriel retrieved it just as he heard the resounding slam of the heavy front door.

He could feel Izzy's perplexed eyes on him but for once there were no ready answers in his head for what had just taken place.

'I can only apologise for that.' He turned to look at her but maintained his distance, watching her carefully. He loathed scenes and, had he had the faintest inkling that Bianca would be descending and on the warpath, he would have taken appropriate diversionary measures.

Of course, he should have expected nothing less. Sacking Bella, her treasured go-between, would have been a red rag to a bull and it was no surprise that she had made sure to arrive at night. As far as Bianca was concerned, it would have been perfect timing to find him with a woman. He had put a dent in her theoretically unassailable armour and it stood to reason that she would want to rebuild her defences as fast as possible.

It was ironic that finding him with Izzy, finding him with Izzy in a compromising situation, had been sheer luck on her part. The truth was that he had never, not once, brought any woman back to his house when Rosa was with him. The very thought was distasteful.

But Bianca was not to know that and now, here he was, stuck between a rock and a hard place.

He could smell the musky scent of spent passion on himself and could see the same thing in Izzy in her wildly tousled hair, her swollen lips and hectic skin, not to mention the casual disarray of her clothes.

There was no doubt in his mind that Bianca would not have missed a single one of those telling signs of two people who had just made love.

'Does your ex-wife make a habit of surprising you in the middle of the night, Gabriel?'

'Do you want a drink? I think I need something strong and stiff. A whisky.'

'I have no intention of being caught up in whatever marital disagreements you might be having with your ex.' Izzy folded her arms and looked at him coldly. 'And, no, I do not want a drink.'

Izzy, still smarting from the insults that had casually been flung at her, could barely move. Her body was stiff, her head was throbbing and she feared that if she tried to take a step forward she would crash to the ground in a heap of broken bits.

Not his usual type...a nondescript little thing...a cheap floozy...

She was angry, humiliated and mortified but most of all she was *hurt*.

Had she just been a convenient plaything for him? Did his tastes lie with types like Bianca—volatile raven-haired beauties with big hair, big breasts and lots of jewellery? For her surprise visit, she had worn a tight red dress, black heels and full make-up. Didn't they say that men tended to run to type, always drawn to versions of the same woman? Had she just been a novelty toy for him to enjoy because they happened to be sharing the same space and she'd made herself available to him?

Lost her virginity to him.

She felt the prick of tears and looked away quickly, but not fast enough, because he had his arms around her before she could think of taking evasive measures.

'How dare you involve me in your drama?' she whispered shakily. 'How dare you imply that we have that sort of relationship because you wanted to get your ex-wife off your back? How *dare* you?'

She pushed him hard and stood back, breathing heavily, looking at him and wishing more than anything that she could hate him. But there he stood and underneath the usually formidably controlled exterior she could see the man who had been shaken, caught off-guard, a prisoner of his love for his daughter which had stopped him from taking control of the situation in a way she knew he had probably wanted to.

There'd been something so enormously *human* about him just then that she could feel her silly heart begin to soften, which just made her even madder.

'You're furious,' Gabriel said, voice barely audible, 'And I don't blame you.' He moved restlessly, raking his fingers through his hair, unable to quite meet her searching, dismayed gaze. 'You're right, of course. I involved you in my personal drama and I had no right to do that. The only excuse I have at my disposal is that I acted purely on impulse. Highly unusual for me, I admit, but then…' He sighed, seemed to consider getting himself that drink, thought better of it and instead took both her hands in his and held her, resisting her efforts to pull away.

'I don't want you to touch me,' she said, but there seemed little point in trying to detach from his iron grip.

'Aside from involving you in something that is not your concern,' he continued, the sincerity in his deep, sexy voice keeping her pinned to the spot, 'I want to apologise for the fact that she insulted you. I would have laid into her, but my darling ex-wife can be explosive when the mood takes her, and I was simply not in the mood for thrown crockery and shrieking that could wake the dead, never mind Rosa. That's the last thing I want to subject my daughter to.

'I've had experiences of that behaviour in the past and there was no way I wanted a repeat performance. She can get…unpredictable when riled. Physical. It's something that has always been at the back of my mind in my dealings with her. If I rile her, how much would she take her frustration and anger out on Rosa? I avoid courting any situation that could…lead to any unfortunate situations. Like most kids, Rosa is loyal. She would never say anything to me. I live with the reality that it is best to avoid inciting potential unpleasantness.'

He paused and said with rough honesty, 'The truth is, between you and Bianca, there is an ocean of difference.'

Izzy did not want to be tempted into hearing what he had to say. 'I don't want excuses and I don't want lies. I think it's time for me to get back to Hawaii and finish the job I started. My brother's been patient but he won't be patient for ever. I've done what I could for Evelyn, and my heart breaks for her, but if you can't be persuaded then there's nothing left I can do.'

'I… I don't want you to go.'

'And I don't care what you want.'

'I can't stop you, Izzy, but…'

'But what, Gabriel?'

'This isn't a conversation to have standing up. Let's go into the sitting room.'

'I'm tired, Gabriel. I just want to go to my bed-room and go to sleep.'

'Please…'

It was so unusual to hear this strong, proud man plead that she hesitated, then nodded without smil-ing and followed him into one of the many sitting rooms on the ground floor.

Like the majority of the rooms in this wing of the mansion, the view was of the vast rows of vines, bearing the grapes that yielded the fine wines that graced so many tables up and down the country. Gabriel moved to snap shut the heavy cream cur-tains then he hesitated and looked to where she was perched formally on one of the sofas.

Finally, he walked towards her and sat close, so that their knees were touching.

Izzy stiffened. With every ounce of willpower inside her, she wanted to ignore the strain etched in his face, but it was hard. He had climbed under her skin, crept into her heart and she felt that she was now conditioned to reach towards him instead of drawing away. And what he had said about his ex-wife and Rosa…how could she fail to be moved?

Gabriel could feel the tension in her. Could he blame her? Not at all. His fury when he thought of Bianca showing up in his house, availing herself of a key she should not have had, was overpowering.

And when he thought of her standing there, ad-dressing Izzy with contempt, he wanted to punch something. He hadn't been lying when he'd said that he knew what sort of scenes his ex was capable of and neither had he been exaggerating when he'd told Izzy that he had endured Rosa being caught in the middle of warfare, baffled and terrified by Bianca in the midst of one of her scenes.

Never again.

He'd remained silent but Izzy deserved more than his silence now.

'I should never have married Bianca,' he confessed, fumbling his way, because discussing feelings and emotions had never been his thing. 'But I did. I suppose part of the attraction was the fact that our backgrounds were so different.'

'How do you mean?'

'I may be able to buy the world now,' he said drily, dark eyes keenly watching the delicate bloom of colour in her cheeks, 'But I came from the wrong side of the tracks. Bianca comes from Italian royalty and at first I found it amusing to be pursued by her. I would have broken up with her, but she fell pregnant, and naturally there was no way I could walk away. We married, but it proved to be a calamitous mistake from day one. By the time Rosa was born, it was clear that everything was unravelling at pace.'

'I'm sorry.' She thought that if the word 'royalty' could be used to define anyone it should be him and not his screaming ex-wife, which just went to show that nobility and dignity could thrive anywhere and in anyone. She itched to question him further about his childhood but remained silent, fighting the temptation to sink right back into him.

Gabriel shrugged and looked at her. 'Why? None of this is your concern, as you made clear.'

Izzy reddened.

'She will use this against me,' Gabriel told her bluntly. 'You leave now, and she will see it as a passport to make things as uncomfortable for me as she can because she will deduce that you were what she expected you to be—a one-night stand, something seedy I allowed to happen while I was in charge of Rosa.'

'We don't live in Victorian times,' Izzy pointed out flatly. 'People actually do continue to have lives post-divorce without hiding those lives away from their kids.'

'It's not so simple for me. At any rate, that's one reason why I would rather you stay. It's selfish, and asking much, but for my daughter I would do anything.' He paused and then said, flushing darkly, 'I would also miss you if you choose to go.'

'You would *miss* me?' Izzy scoffed. Their eyes met and she held his dark gaze with difficulty. It was hard maintaining her tough stance. Was this what love did to you? she floundered desperately. What was the point of it if it turned you into a rag doll, at the mercy of someone you wanted to walk away from? Gabriel didn't love her. That should have been her cue to turn her back and leave after that uncomfortable scene, but she was still nailed to the spot, and when she thought about walking away she quailed inside.

'I would miss you, Izzy.' He looked at her in silence for a few moments. 'Can I offer you a deal?'

He would miss her. There was a simplicity to that statement that chipped away at her weak defences.

He didn't love her but there was something there. She felt it. Surely it couldn't be just her imagination?

'A deal?' Her mind was still busy with the prospect of the void opening at her feet, because go she would have to. Wouldn't she?

'Stay…just until I sort various things out with Bianca…and I will guarantee the cottage.'

'Come again?'

'I have things in place to finally deal with Bianca, to put us on an even footing. She has plans to remove Rosa to Tuscany. She will use whatever means she can to facilitate that, if that's what she decides to do, and she will enjoy the process. Stay and I will guarantee in writing that your friend will be able to end her days where she is in peace. I will cancel all plans to develop the land around the cottage.'

'Why is she so vindictive? You must have felt something for one another at one time…how did it get to the point where you tell me that she'll stop at nothing to even scores with you? What did you do to her?'

* * *

Gabriel shifted and frowned, primed to resent the intrusion into his personal life.

With a trace of unease, he acknowledged that she had already crashed through barriers other women had baulked at and hastily retreated from. He wondered when that trend had started and how it was that he hadn't knocked her back sooner. It was what he did…

However, he had to concede that he had already told her so much that clarifying his disastrous marriage added little to the equation. Besides, if he were to get her on board then he would have to meet her halfway when it came to telling her what she wanted to know.

And what was the big deal, anyway? She deserved answers to her very natural curiosity. He trusted her with Rosa. He could trust her with a few incidental details of his past.

'I failed to give her the level of attention she needed,' Gabriel said eventually. He sat back and for a few seconds closed his eyes, then he pressed his thumbs on them in a gesture of extreme weariness. 'Bianca…' he turned to Izzy, thoughtful '… was brought up to expect the world to bow to her and men, in particular, had a duty to put her ahead of everything.'

'And you didn't?'

'Not didn't. *Couldn't.*'

'What do you mean?'

'When you grow up without anything you learn fast that what matters is money,' he said flatly. 'Not because it can buy you this…' He glanced around at the sitting room with its priceless works of art, its expensive furnishings, its cool glass-and-marble décor. 'But because it can buy you respect and freedom. I am untouchable, for want of a better word.'

'You swapped the joy of love for the respect of other people? Strangers?'

'I consider it a fair trade.' He shrugged. 'At any rate she decided that, if she couldn't get the attention she craved from me, then she would look elsewhere. Divorce rapidly followed, and here we are several years later.'

'You would back off from selling the land… Evelyn would be able to relax, knowing that she wouldn't be pressured to sell?'

'You have my word.'

'Despite the fact that it'll mean giving up what you want?'

'I'm at the top of the food chain. I can afford the loss.'

'Then why didn't you offer to do that before?'

'Because I'm not Father Christmas.'

So ruthless, Izzy thought, so cold. Yet so impossibly *human* and so incredibly, compellingly *complex*.

He had dangled the biggest carrot in front of her and she knew that she should resent his blackmail. But then she thought of spending a bit more time with him and she couldn't fight the weakness inside her that *wanted* those crumbs.

He couldn't love, he said. His life experiences had propelled him into locking away his heart and throwing away the key, he said.

But they *had* something. Maybe he had just married the wrong woman…

She impatiently swept that thought out of her head and said coolly, 'I'll have to think about it.'

'This is a once-in-a-lifetime offer,' Gabriel countered. 'I need your decision now.'

'How long would we…?'

'You make it sound as though I'm backing you into a corner where nothing short of a bed of nails awaits. I'm not.' This time, when he looked at her, there was an intimacy in his eyes that had the predictable effect on her disobedient body.

Just like that he could arouse her, fill her head with images of them together naked, his hands on her bare skin, his mouth exploring her in ways that made her cry out with pleasure.

'You're blackmailing me,' she protested weakly.

'I'm giving you options. What's your answer?'

'You still haven't told me how long you think this…er…arrangement will last. What is going to change?'

Gabriel lowered his eyes. Knowledge was power, he thought, musing on all the information he had managed to glean. But that was something he had no intention of imparting. Not least because he had not quite managed to square it with his conscience, however many times he'd tried to justify everything to himself.

With things in motion, he would have a way forward and a timeline, and it would be immensely satisfying. It would take many weeks to get to the final destination, but to get to that vital place where Bianca accepted his authority, in receipt of everything he now had to show her...*days*.

'No more than a fortnight.'

'A fortnight.'

'Like I said, Izzy...' He reached forward to gently trail his finger along her wrist before moving it in tiny circles with devastating effect. 'Two weeks isn't going to be a hardship for me. Will it be for you?'

Izzy tried hard to quell the rising tide of desire inside her. She stared at that brown finger moving against her paler skin and sternly told herself to think *practically*. Two weeks and Evelyn's future would be secured. Was that too great a sacrifice?

No. And he was right. The chemistry between them was undeniable. Two weeks would give her time to adjust to the changes ahead, prepare her for when she had to walk away, go back to Hawaii. Time to pin him down on dates and give herself a vital timeline, she said to herself with the cool logic of someone weighing up the pros and cons and arriving at a decision with thought and good judgement.

'You're right.' Love was something to be hidden away with him. There was no point trying to analyse the whens and whys and how she had managed so completely to fall under his spell. Nor was there any point in telling him that she no longer wanted to be his lover. She did. She still wanted him. He gave her goose bumps and she couldn't think of him, far less look at him, without wanting to touch him.

She knew that she would do what it took for Evelyn to be safe for the rest of her days, and she also knew that it would be no hardship for her either.

But she had to exert some control over the situation. Why should he be the one calling all the shots?

'So you'll stay…a while…?' He smiled a slow, curling smile that threatened to wash away all her resolve.

'A while.' Izzy looked at him with composure. 'I resent being dragged into a situation with your ex-wife, but I do care about Rosa very much, and wouldn't want to see her hurt in any way if it's true what you've said about Bianca.'

'You have my word that the woman would stop at nothing to get her own back at me. Believe me, Izzy, there's no way under the sun I would ever involve you or anyone else in my private life if I had a choice.'

Well, doesn't that say it all? Izzy thought. Left to his own devices, this would only have been about sex, but fate had decided to intervene, and here he was, having to share a sliver of his past with her, grudgingly and resentfully.

Had she ever thought that she would willingly hand her heart over to a man who wasn't interested in love? Who was happy to admit that he had no intention of ever forming any serious and committed relationship with anyone? Especially after Jefferson and the devastating sense of betrayal she had felt at the time. And yet she had, and she could no more make sense of herself than she could figure out how to build a rocket and fly to the moon.

'And I care even more about Evelyn. Her safety and security means the world to me. If I'm to go ahead with this arrangement, then I want your agreement in writing, signed and witnessed by the appropriate parties.'

'You don't trust me?'

'Maybe in this short space of time I've learnt from the master that trust is a commodity not to be taken for granted.' She met his eyes squarely and he scowled in return, withdrawing his hand, leaving behind a coolness she hated. She clasped her hands together and kept her eyes pinned to his handsome face.

Did he have the right to dish out homilies about trusting no one…because *trust* was a hindrance when the only thing you cared about was making money so that the rest of the world could bow at your feet…while expecting *her* to trust everything he said as the gospel truth?

The galling thing was that she *did* trust him, absolutely and completely. He was as good as his word, and she had the grace to blush at what she had just imparted, even though it was just part and parcel of approaching the situation in as detached a manner as possible.

'Of course,' Gabriel countered politely. 'I'll have everything signed and above board. No room for me taking advantage of you.'

'That's not what I meant.'

'No?'

'I also need to call my brother. He's been patient with me taking time out here to try and sort Evelyn's affairs but he's only going to be patient for so long. I'm going to phone him tomorrow and tell him that I'll be back in Hawaii in exactly two weeks' time.' Keen to break the sudden tension, and smiling hesitantly as she reached out for the hand that had just left hers, she added, 'Max isn't the most patient person on the planet.'

Gabriel shrugged. 'That's fair enough,' he agreed, matching her conciliatory smile with one of his own. 'It's late. Let's go upstairs.'

They made love. Again. It was late, and they were tired, but the bed was a soothing haven after hours spent in what seemed to Izzy some kind of parallel universe.

The following morning, Izzy took Rosa into town for ice-cream, and when she returned a little before lunch a lawyer was there and papers had been drawn up for signature.

Gabriel had taken her at her word. She'd demanded everything be done by the book, and he was adhering to that request to the letter.

She signed the papers, Rosa having been dispatched to watch television.

The lawyer was a formally dressed middle-aged man, and everything had been prepared meticulously and explained to her in even more scrupulous detail.

To one side, Gabriel watched, having scrawled his signature on the papers. Flustered and hot after a morning spent in town, Izzy was very much aware of his towering presence behind her.

This felt so formal. They might be lovers, she thought in self-defence, but that didn't mean he owed her anything. If things didn't work out between he and his ex-wife, whatever those *things* might be, then who was to say he wouldn't try to justify reneging on his word?

He never would. But she clung to that very sensible deduction as, finally, the last page was signed and she went to return the pen to the lawyer.

'Not so fast.'

Izzy looked at Gabriel, bemused, and he nodded to the lawyer who produced two sheets of paper, impeccably typed and formatted as the rest had been.

'What's that?' she asked, surprised.

'The issue of trust cuts both ways,' he said drily.

'You want to ensure my promise is legally binding and I, likewise, want to ensure that your promise is legally binding as well...'

Izzy read the document. It was brief. A fortnight bound to his side with no leeway for a change of heart.

Of course. Why not? But for him, there were different motivations. Whilst she had insisted on all the dots and crosses being in the right place, because she had been desperate to assume the mantle of someone detached dealing with an unexpected development in a business-like manner, *he* would have done the same because he was not attached to her in any way, aside from the physical.

Whist she was pretending to be in charge, he wasn't pretending anything at all. They might be lovers, but a deal was a deal, and she suspected that even if she hadn't insisted on anything being signed *he* would not have been quite so trusting.

She signed, but her eyes were stinging.

Had the lawyer noticed anything? What must he make of this peculiar arrangement? He was obviously well-trained, because his expression betrayed nothing as he gathered the various papers, exchanged a few pleasantries and then left, shown to the front door by Gabriel while Izzy waited in the sitting room.

Why did it hurt so much that he'd made her sign a piece of paper? Was she so naïve to believe that there would be one rule for her and another for him? It felt as though something jarring had been introduced between them, and she wondered how she would be able to relax with him if she knew, at the back of her mind, that he didn't trust her. Yet hadn't her own actions suggested the very same thing to him?

She didn't notice Gabriel back at the door. She was trying to talk herself into an upbeat frame of mind.

Gabriel stilled for a few seconds, looking at her staring through the bay window, half-turned away. Her hands were balled into fists and her body language shrieked unhappiness.

He knew why.

He'd asked her to sign a piece of paper, just as she had asked him to, but his request had cut her to the quick. If he hadn't been as in control of his life as he was, then he might have been tempted to think that her demand for transparency from him was equally cutting, but he decided that any response along those lines was beneath him.

Still, her posture punctured his usual formidable cool and he was tempted to make amends in some way or another.

He scowled, because since when was it in his nature to placate where placating was not necessary? He cleared his throat and strolled towards her.

'Happy?' he asked, circling around so that she was compelled to look at him. How could she look so enticing and so utterly seductive when she was wearing no more than some faded dungarees with a white vest underneath and flip-flops, and had her hair tied back in a pony tail, face bare of all make-up? She was so endearingly fresh-faced, so lacking in artifice. He recalled that first time, finding out that she was a virgin, and the drive to make her smile again was like the physical twist of something sharp inside him.

His reaction bewildered him but he didn't stop to analyse why.

She shrugged and offered him a weak smile. 'Yep. All signed. Evelyn will be overjoyed to find out that she can stay in the cottage. She puts on a brave front but she's had so many sleepless nights...' Her voice tapered off and her eyes skittered away from his. 'I should go and see about fixing Rosa some lunch.'

'Rosa can wait a couple of minutes,' Gabriel told her gruffly. He raked his fingers through his hair and fidgeted. 'You *did* ask for everything to be legally documented,' he pointed out.

'I did. Yes.'

'So why do you look as though the tooth fairy forgot to leave a quarter under the pillow?'

'Do I? I'm sorry.' She tried on a smile for size. 'I'm really happy that everything's sorted.'

'I'm sorry. I should not have asked you to sign that piece of paper.'

Izzy's eyes flew to his. Her heart skipped a beat because this was not what she had expected. Apologies didn't come easy to a guy like Gabriel and the roughened undertone to his voice said it all. He was uncomfortable saying sorry and the apology was all the more heartfelt for that.

'I was hurt,' Izzy confessed simply. 'And I know I shouldn't have been. I asked you to make sure everything was legal so why shouldn't you do the same with me?'

'Because,' Gabriel told her heavily, 'The situation wasn't the same at all. You needed clarity on something that had to be legally binding with no room for a change of heart, and you were quite right to have insisted on that. I am a businessman, after all. I have learnt to take nothing for granted. Whereas…'

He looked away for a few seconds then returned his dark gaze to her face. 'Whereas there was no such necessity from me. There was no need for you to sign anything because you are not committed to doing anything for me that goes against your conscience or puts you in any position you feel is uncomfortable.'

Gabriel realised, with surprise, that whilst he'd presumed all to be fair in love and war, whilst he should feel no compunction about asking her to stick around until he sorted Bianca, having abandoned his lucrative deal to get her on board, he actually did feel ashamed. Buying her compliance shouldn't make him feel ever so slightly soiled, but it did. Money, it would seem, couldn't buy whatever you wanted after all.

'You just had to ask,' Izzy told him gently. 'I hate the thought of Rosa being used as a pawn because your ex-wife has an axe to grind. I would have agreed to stay on for a couple of weeks either way. I'm not heartless.'

'No. You're anything but.' He smiled. 'Kiss and make up?'

Izzy's heart soared. Relief that peace between them had been restored was overwhelming. 'Kiss and make up,' she agreed.

For now…

But the present would soon become the future and then…the kisses would come to an end.

The clock was ticking. She knew it and she knew that he did as well…

CHAPTER NINE

'I HAVE SOME NEWS.' Izzy smiled drowsily and twirled the stem of the wine glass in her hand.

It was a warm night. Above them, the sky was black velvet, studded with a million stars. Here, in the gazebo Gabriel had arranged the evening before—because he was sick of eating indoors and neither of them thought it was fair to impose on Evelyn to babysit—she felt like royalty.

This likely had something to do with the huge Egyptian cushions on which they were sitting, not to mention the silver cutlery, the crystal wine-glasses and the fine bone-China plates on which the remains of their main course were awaiting collection by the waiter hired for the evening. They were having a selection of finger foods prepared by one of the local chefs and the very best Sauvignon from the grapes of Gabriel's vineyard. On the ground, four over-sized lanterns provided pools of mellow light and there were strings of fairy lights entwined on the sides of the gazebo.

It was breathtakingly romantic, although when she'd mentioned that earlier Gabriel had laughed and said he'd commissioned the thing to appear at a designated time, not chosen it himself.

Still…

The past five days had been dreamy. It was almost as if this weird deal had opened up another door between them…had given them permission for what they had to deepen.

At least, that was what Izzy cared to think. She loved him and keenly noticed every small gesture he made, every sideways glance, every passing smile.

And, now that he had explained about Bianca, she felt that there was a bond between them, even though he'd never recognise anything of the sort. He wouldn't. It wasn't his way. When it came to anything to do with feelings or emotions, he resolutely took the same line. Whilst she was sure he firmly believed the stories he told himself about not being able to feel, surely there was something there, something strong and binding?

Izzy knew that she was treading on dangerous ground just thinking like that but she couldn't help herself.

'What's that?'

'My brother is getting married. I spoke to him this morning. I could scarcely believe it but he's marrying my friend Mia.'

'When's the big day?' Gabriel asked, stifling a

yawn, and Izzy nudged him with her toe. He couldn't possibly fall asleep. It was way too beautiful out here.

'In a month's time. They're going to go to London to have a look at places to buy just outside it—he said that Mia isn't interested in the frantic pace of big city life. And they're going to divide their time between Hawaii and England.'

'Interesting.'

Izzy laughed languidly. He was half-lying, propping himself up. He'd complained about the low seating arrangement in the gazebo but had burst out laughing when she'd told him not to be boring. Tapas wasn't meant to be eaten at a table sitting upright on uncomfortable chairs.

He'd kissed her long and slowly until she'd been trembling all over and half-wishing that they were near a bed instead of under the night skies.

While she had gone all out and was wearing a floaty, flowery silk dress with thin straps and sandals, the very opposite of anything she'd normally consider wearing, he was in a pair of faded jeans, a T-shirt and some loafers.

The waiter emerged from the shadows to remove the plates and reappeared minutes later with a silver platter groaning under the weight of tiny desserts, exquisitely made and begging to be eaten.

'I shall have to email Mia to get all the gory details,' Izzy went on, slipping down so that she could nestle in the crook of his arm, leaving the desserts for a while. He was staring out towards the dark sky and so was she. His house was within sight, just, but it still felt as though they were the only two people in the world.

'I'm picturing a ten-page email.' His voice was low and amused. 'Might be a better idea to call...'

'There *would* be a lot of questions,' Izzy agreed, grinning. 'You're right about a phone call. I wonder if James knows? I guess he must... I'll have to find out.'

'I want to make love to you right here, right now. How does that sound to you?' Gabriel murmured, angling his big body so that he could kiss her.

'Is sex all you ever think about?' Izzy teased, but she curved against him, angling back so that she could trail little kisses against his neck as she slipped her hand underneath his T-shirt, thrilling to the feel of solid, packed muscle. 'Besides, we can't do anything out here. Don't forget, there's a very attentive waiter in residence.'

And remember the last time we were surprised in a state of disarray, she was almost tempted to add. She didn't think her blood pressure could stand anyone else catching her *in flagrante delicto*, so to speak.

'I'm paying for that attentive waiter,' Gabriel drawled. 'He'll do whatever I tell him to do.'

'Yes, but what on earth would he think?'

'Yes,' Gabriel mimicked, half-laughing. 'But why on earth would you care?'

He gave the waiter instructions that they were not

to be disturbed under any circumstances, short of his daughter waking up or the house burning down.

He pushed aside the tray with the tasty titbits. He pushed the silver wine cooler to one side and then he tenderly semi-undressed her, instinctively seeming to know that she would feel more comfortable if she weren't in a state of complete undress.

There was something exquisitely thoughtful about that, a subconscious act of consideration that warmed her heart.

Their sex was stupendous. With him she had dropped all her inhibitions—had even gone on the pill so that neither of them had to worry about an unexpected accident—but she was still shy when it came to nudity and he had clocked that without her ever having to say.

He slipped the straps of her dress down and methodically undid all twelve pearl buttons down the front so that he could suckle on her breasts, swirling his tongue across her nipples as she moaned softly, eyes closed, her hand behind his dark head.

Around them, the breeze whispered through the acres of vines, and the shadows of little flying insects were exaggerated around the lanterns and fairy lights.

They made love quietly. When his hand slipped under her panties to sink into her wetness, she felt her muscles contract, and small ripples of pleasure grew longer and fiercer, from ripples to waves, until she was so close to coming that she had to squeeze shut her legs and focus on just hanging on for a bit longer.

He didn't strip off his T-shirt but he shoved his jeans down, unzipping them unsteadily, kicking them off. Then he tugged off her panties and came inside, filling her, stretching her until she was soaring and clasping him tightly against her.

Their bodies were slick with perspiration and their grunts of satisfaction were muted, which added to a certain sizzling excitement. They were two teenagers making out in the back of a car, even though Izzy had never had that experience first-hand, so she could only surmise.

Afterwards, sated, they lay back. Izzy wriggled her dress back on, he climbed into his jeans and then he drew her towards him and haphazardly began pointing out various constellations, some with silly names, obviously made up to make her giggle.

She talked to him about Max and growing up. She'd dipped into that conversation on a few occasions now, revealing a little more about herself with each foray.

He asked her about her brothers, and she laughed and told him that she'd always been closer to James, who was relaxed, easygoing and instantly charming in a way Max had never been.

'Although,' she said pensively, 'Who knows how he's changed since he's fallen in love and is full of the joys of getting married?' She paused and then said cautiously, 'You could come to the wedding with me. If you like.'

Silence greeted this and Izzy could have kicked herself. Everything had been going so well.

'Just a thought,' she added hastily. 'Crazy, considering I'll be well gone by then! We will both have moved on.'

Gabriel didn't have to see her face to know exactly what was going on in her head. Was it so far-fetched? Here they were, having a great time—why should they be compelled to limit their enjoyment to a two-week period? Things were in place with regard to Bianca. He had consulted a top lawyer, handing over all the evidence at his disposal. It seemed that he would have no problem in levelling the playing field, if not taking it over completely, fencing it off and putting up a sign that trespassers, in the form of his dearest ex-wife, would be prosecuted. Her parenting was borderline negligent and he had the proof to present.

Izzy didn't want to tread on any toes by presuming anything and he really liked that about her. She was funny, smart, touchingly disingenuous, forthright and she had never, not once, overstepped the mark.

Not once had she asked anything of him that she knew he would be unwilling to give, do or say.

'I could think about it…'

* * *

He tucked her neatly against him and stroked her cheek with his finger. Izzy felt a surge of pure bliss.

'Really?'

'Really,' Gabriel murmured huskily. 'Why not?'

'Well…this charade has a timeline, remember? Two weeks. We're well into week one. Max and Mia won't be getting married for another month.'

'There are exceptions to everything,' Gabriel returned silkily. 'Timelines included. I'm enjoying this—I'm enjoying *you*—so why should I limit myself to a two-week curfew?'

Izzy snuggled against him, heart soaring. That small victory felt huge. Life had become a roller-coaster ride and right now she was at the height of the arc, swooping into the heavens and loving the euphoria.

Soon after, they tidied themselves up and headed back into the house. The catering staff would clear up behind them. The tiny desserts hadn't been touched, but she'd been too distracted to remember them.

It had been the perfect evening.

She hadn't been expecting it and the mere fact that he had done something so wildly impulsive had appealed to her romantic heart in ways she could scarcely vocalise, even to herself. It was all the more impressive because it was the sort of thing she would never have associated with him. He was so coolly logical, so fond of keeping his emotional distance… The gesture had felt strangely significant, even though she fought hard to bank down that impression.

And now…he'd agreed to attend Max and Mia's wedding with her. For someone who was resolutely proud of his inability to love, surely a wedding should be the last event he would agree to attend?

But they would be together, still an item, no more time limit on their relationship. That elevated it from being a business arrangement, which had felt so strange, to something entirely different and she couldn't help but want to savour the difference.

Was she being an idiot? Probably, she mused happily, but since when was it a crime to be an idiot?

They hit the house and both went up to check on Rosa, with Izzy hanging back by the door, half-watching him as he leant down to kiss his daughter and gently pull the covers back over her, half-thinking about how everything had changed for her in such a short space of time.

She waited for him, hovering, kissed him once he'd half-shut Rosa's door and then turned away to head back to her own bedroom suite.

'The night's not over yet.' He tugged her to him, hooked his arm behind her back and kissed her long and deeply, his tongue meshing with hers and instantly making her body forget that they had only just made love, that she should be sated and ready to sleep.

They made it to his bedroom, semi-entwined, and were already stripping off as the door shut behind them. He pressed her against the door, pinning her with his mouth and his hands, his knee nudging between her legs, opening them, pressing against her crotch until she was whimpering and as weak as a rag doll.

The wispy summer dress, only just back on, was stripped off in under a minute and she wrenched off her panties as he did the same with his clothes.

Neither had bothered to switch on the light but the bank of white floor-to-ceiling shutters were open and the breeze sifting through was cool.

They staggered naked, wrapped up in one another, barely making progress until he hefted her off her feet and strode towards the bed.

She was halfway to coming and so was he when he entered her in one deep, powerful thrust. She felt his release just as hers swept her away, wrenching a long, guttural cry from her lips and leaving her utterly and wonderfully shattered afterwards.

The fierceness of this love-making…the decadent night time picnic under a starry sky…his husky admission that he no more wanted this to end than she did…was all adding up to something that felt very much like love. For a few perilous seconds, she gave herself over to imagining what it would feel like for this relationship to veer off on a tangent he might not anticipate into a world for which he had no road map.

Lazily, she felt herself dozing off, but not for long,

because he ran her a bath and it was another forty minutes before she yawned and sleepily kissed him on the mouth.

'Don't go.' Standing by the door, he buried his face in her hair. Her arms were wrapped round him. He pulled back and looked down at her, and in the shadows his face was an arrangement of beautiful angles. 'Stay the night…'

Later, Izzy was to think that habit was the enemy of caution. That first night together heralded the beginning of nights spent together.

A routine was established. Gabriel reluctantly returned to his work, having spent several days doing all manner of family-orientated activities. The three of them would breakfast together, usually outside, and then he would disappear, leaving Rosa and her to busy themselves, which they very happily did. They explored the vineyards, went on day trips and shopped in the small, pretty town.

They often went to visit Evelyn, who had a renewed bounce to her step now that the hangman's noose had been removed from around her neck. Often, she and Rosa would lose themselves in planting something or other, with Evelyn meticulously explaining everything about whatever plant they happened to be handling. Izzy would sit in one of the deck chairs in Evelyn's back garden, her thoughts at last turning to the job she had left behind.

She would have to go back but she wanted to

know that the parameters of her role had changed. No longer would she be dealing with the business side of things, the very side she was so qualified to deal with, given her degree. Max had emailed her suggestions as to what her responsibilities might be, and she had tweaked a few areas, but was pleased to know that the creativity that had lain buried for so many years would be allowed free rein.

She would design the layout of the hotel and the cottages which would be nestled amongst the trees. She would be responsible for sourcing everything that went into making them unique, from wall hangings to artists who could produce the murals and furniture made from the various local woods she envisaged for some of the spaces. With the hotel no longer to be luxury five-star but luxury eco, she envisaged a completely different bias to her job, one she was very much looking forward to bringing to fruition.

And how would Gabriel slot in?

Izzy didn't spend time thinking about the details. She was happy to accept the fact that they now shared something, a bond that would bypass whatever inconveniences might rear their irritating heads. After all, didn't they say that where there was a will, there was a way?

And it felt like they were a team, the three of them. She, Gabriel and Rosa…

Gabriel stopped work at six without fail, if not earlier, and engaged with this daughter in a way Izzy admired. The business with Bianca had been satisfactorily sorted. He didn't go into details, merely informing her when she asked that his ex had finally had a taste of the medicine she had been so keen to dish out before.

And they made love. Spectacular, wonderful love that more and more persuaded her that the chemistry between them ran so much deeper than he probably thought. Yes, shimmering on less rosy horizons lurked the uncomfortable reality that for him, whilst not for her, chemistry might be something quite detached from anything else. After all, had he ever, even in the throes of passion, mentioned *love*? Wasn't it always easy to believe what you wanted to believe? The pictures and possibilities she had conjured could be oh, so different from the ones he had, and she knew that somewhere deep inside her she was scared to find out.

She was absently watching Evelyn and Rosa meticulously patting down earth into bright-blue flowerpots when she heard the ping of her phone.

And there it was.

The timely reminder that the very minute you began to take things for granted, to allow yourself to enjoy life and nurture expectations that your enjoyment might actually last, fate stepped in to shatter the daydream.

It was no more than a short text but from the very last person on earth she expected to hear from.

Why was Bianca texting her? Why did she want

to meet up? What the heck could the other woman have to say to her? She would be in town, the other woman said, and she thought it would be mutually beneficial for them to have a chat. *How could either of them have anything to say to one another that could be mutually beneficial?*

Should she say something to Gabriel?

A place was suggested.

Izzy was shaking ever so slightly as she shoved her phone back into the rucksack she took with her everywhere.

Why would she bother Gabriel with this nonsense? It was ten in the morning. He would be sequestered in his office, working, and would be there all day until he broke off in the early evening. It was his routine. Lunch was brought to him, barely causing a ripple in his working day. What would be the point in disturbing him?

Two o'clock was suggested. It would be easy enough to leave Rosa with Evelyn.

Izzy only hesitated for a few seconds, then she extracted the phone and texted back.

Okay.

The meeting place surprised Izzy because it wasn't the fanciest place in town. After a mere five minutes' acquaintance, she suspected the other woman was really only comfortable somewhere expensive and pretentious, where wall-to-wall waiter service was on tap at the click of an imperious finger.

This was more of a café, busy and pretty, nestling alongside a collection of shops and boutiques, all of which lazed under a portico interrupted by a series of jade-green columns.

The city of Napa, Izzy had discovered, was made for picture-perfect snapshots, with the impressionistic backdrop of hazy, lavender hills in the distance as far as the eye could see.

It was warm and sunny, and the pavements were busy. Izzy had dressed smart-casually. She'd ditched the jeans in favour of a pair of trousers and a short-sleeved blouse, which was neatly tucked into the waistband, and some tan sandals.

Bianca was unmissable in the café. Eyes down as she scrolled through her phone, she was in a tight peacock-blue mini-dress, precariously high heels and a wealth of jewellery.

Proceed with caution, Izzy thought as she took a deep breath and headed towards the table.

She had to clear her throat before the other woman glanced up, and even then she made a show of blinking in puzzlement, as though startled by the appearance of a perfect stranger at her table.

'You came, my dear. I had my doubts.'

'I haven't got long, Bianca.' Izzy slipped into the chair and adjusted it slightly so that she was a few inches further away from Bianca.

'And I wouldn't dream of keeping you. Perhaps

you need to hurry back to play at being the dutiful girlfriend to my ex-husband?'

Izzy reddened but was saved from a response by the appearance of a pretty young waitress.

'A coffee... No, nothing to eat.'

The sooner she got this over and done with, the better.

'So…' Bianca leaned forward in a waft of expensive perfume and her expression was hard. 'I am assuming Gabriel has kept you in the loop about his… recent attacks on me? No?'

'What point are you going to make, Bianca? I really can't sit around here playing games with you.'

'The point I am making, my dear little thing, is that you really shouldn't trust my ex-husband. You might be engaged, although I don't see a ring on your finger, but it won't last.'

'I don't have to sit here and listen to this.'

'But you do, dear child, because I only have your wellbeing at heart.'

'Thank you for that.' Izzy smiled sweetly, gearing up to get to her feet and leave as fast as she could. 'I'll treasure it for ever.'

Bianca's coal-black eyes glittered with menace and she reached out to circle Izzy's wrist with her fingers.

Dismayed, Izzy froze, her cornflower blue eyes widening. Inbred politeness compelled her to stay put, but her heart was beating like a sledgehammer and her head was throbbing.

'Gabriel has suddenly come by a great deal of information about my movements,' she hissed. 'About my whereabouts. He had always made a stupidly big deal about making sure to keep Rosa out of our private battles, and I can attest to this because Bella has been my trusted confidante for many years.'

'You mean *spy*? And would you mind releasing me? I don't want to have to create a scene.' Izzy could think of nothing worse, but the threat worked, because Bianca removed her hand and smiled a small, vicious smile.

'Gabriel will have obtained his information from someone, my dear. I have looked at the paperwork and all the relevant dates and it would seem that a little birdie has been whispering all sorts of things in his ear while Bella has been away. All sorts of things he has duly noted and had followed up by a team of investigators. I believe my saintly ex will be able to say, with his hand on his heart, that he learned nothing from Rosa—because someone else has been feeding him information.'

Colour was slowly draining from Izzy's face. *Pillow talk*. And not even specifically pillow talk. Just talk. Mixed in with the laughter, the anecdotes, the stories of her life and the winding tales of what she and Rosa got up to when he wasn't around… Yes, there had been asides…things said to her about Bianca and her unusual style of parenting.

She couldn't put her finger on exactly what had been said but she knew that Rosa had said stuff, head bent as she concentrated on drawing a flower or doing a piece of homework or just sitting alongside her as they played on her games console. She'd talked about the way she often skipped school to go somewhere frivolous with her mother...or was told to disappear because one of Bianca's *friends* might be turning up for a *sleepover*.

'Well!' Bianca reached for the clutch bag on the table, withdrew some bills and left them by her coffee cup. 'Just something to think about, my dear.' She stood up but then immediately leant over and whispered in Izzy's ear. 'As soon as Gabriel has everything he wants, he'll wave goodbye. He used you, dear, and believe me, I *hate* to be the one to have to tell you this. I was going to visit Rosa, but tell her I won't be making it today. So lovely to have this chat. We should do it again some time!'

In a state of shock, Izzy watched Bianca's sashaying departure from the coffee shop.

She couldn't recall making it back to the house. Her head was in a spin. She'd had no idea what she'd expected when she'd agreed to meet the other woman but she should have known that it wouldn't have been fun or relaxing. She'd just been inside a lion's den and she felt nauseous at the revelations Bianca had laid at her door.

Had she been used? She tried to think back, to follow the pattern of their relationship so that she could discover the answer to that question, but the harder she tried, the more confused and upset she became.

The meeting had lasted only minutes. She let herself quietly into the house. She would fetch Rosa later but for now…

She made her way to the far wing of the house, straight to the sprawling space where Gabriel worked. It had everything, from a dedicated work space to a vast sitting area and, of course, a luxurious bathroom suite. A billionaire's home office.

She didn't knock. She pushed open the door, walked right in and, not caring that he was on a call, said, 'I think we need to have a talk.'

This was the first time Izzy had walked into his office without knocking. Gabriel concluded his conference call immediately, then he sat back in his leather chair and looked at her, head tilted to one side, for once not knowing what the hell was going on.

And into that very brief silence Izzy said without inflexion in her voice at all, 'Guess who I just met for coffee?'

Gabriel's eyes narrowed and he watched as she moved forward to subside into the chair in front of him. She was flushed and her bright-blue eyes were shiny, glittering. She'd roped her long hair back into a loose braid and it hung over her shoulder.

He began joining the dots.

'What did she say to you?' he asked, without bothering to beat around the bush.

Bianca had been cornered and had done what she did best—she'd gone for the jugular. In this instance, however, the jugular did not belong to him.

His face revealed nothing, but it was an effort, because inside red-hot fury at his ex-wife was running through his veins like molten lava.

Thanks to what he had learnt, to the people he had commissioned to provide the proof he needed of her negligent parenting, he had his ex on the run. And it was at just the right point in time, because he had discovered she hadn't been bluffing when she had told him about her intention to remove Rosa from the US and take her back to Tuscany, which she had summarily decided was her 'natural home'.

Bianca's mother had got herself involved with a younger man, it would seem, and Bianca had no intention of allowing her inheritance to fall into the wrong hands. Filial duty had suddenly morphed into daughterly love.

With those plans in disarray, it was little wonder she had decided to wreak whatever revenge she could, making sure to keep far away from him. He suspected the nature of the retribution and his blood ran cold.

'How could you, Gabriel?' Izzy whispered.

'Tell me what it is I am supposed to have done.'

'You know what!' She sprang to her feet, as though suddenly unable to remain still, and paced the room in jerky steps before spinning round to look at him with hostile accusation. 'You *used* me.

You pretended… You made me think… All because you wanted me to tell you what Rosa said to me.'

He lowered his eyes, shielding his expression. When he raised them to look at her, he knew his face was shuttered, revealing nothing.

'I didn't use you, Izzy. You're looking at signposts but misreading the signs.'

'What does *that* mean?'

'You should calm down.'

'Don't you *dare* tell me to calm down. You used me to get what you wanted and I *hate* you for that!'

Gabriel felt himself flush as all the chickens came home to roost, except…had he used her? No, he hadn't. He had been the passive recipient of useful information and why was anything wrong with that? She'd taken what Bianca had said and was twisting it into something that sat like something ugly and sharp on his conscience.

He clamped down hard on any inappropriate feelings of guilt. She said that he'd 'made her think…' Made her think *what*? That he *loved* her? Was that the conclusion of that unfinished sentence?

Had he taken his eye off the ball? Encouraged her to have feelings for him? Even though she must surely know, because he had been utterly upfront that he wasn't in it for the long term.

And now she was here, hurling accusations at him, screaming, shouting and tearful.

Was this what he wanted, needed? No. He'd never had time for demanding women with chaotic feelings that needed to be nurtured. He'd learnt the hard way that the only thing that mattered was the cold logic of making money. He'd been lazy and now it was time to say goodbye.

Something inside twisted. He ignored it. Control over lust…*that* was the bottom line…and if he'd forgotten that for a while, then it was time he remembered.

He stood up and moved towards her, paused to meet her fierce blue eyes.

'Don't get on the moral high ground with me,' he said darkly. 'Your friend is sitting pretty in her cottage. No more pressuring Evelyn to sell her home. Some might say that *that* is what using is all about.'

'It's just not the same, Gabriel.'

'Explain the difference.'

'If you can't see it for yourself—' her voice was subdued and she was already half-turning towards the door '—then you never will. Tell Rosa goodbye from me. She's with Evelyn.'

She walked out without looking back.

CHAPTER TEN

G ABRIEL WEARILY RUBBED his eyes, swivelled his chair and stared out of the window of his office.

The view was somewhat different from the one he had had a fortnight ago. No symmetrical, gently swaying vines marching into a distant lavender-hued horizon… No charming local town with a pace of life as slow and steady as a snail's progress across the grass… No pleasing sight of a flat, blue infinity pool waiting to soothe at the end of a hot day.

No very many things, come to think of it.

No Izzy sharing his bed every night… No hearing the sound of her laughter… No walking with Rosa tucked between them asking a million questions… No unwinding at the end of the day with a glass of wine and the soothing backdrop of Izzy's soft voice.

No, that particular bubble had burst, and of course it had always been going to burst.

He was back in New York. The view from the skyscraper that housed his offices looked down at matchstick-sized crowds scuttling frantically across gridlocked streets with everything buried beneath the haze of exhaust fumes and pollution.

Or so it seemed. Everything had changed for him with Rosa, and he told himself that that was the main thing.

Currently, she was with Bianca in Tuscany for two weeks, with a nanny of his choice in attendance. When she returned to America, she would be with him. He was now the one holding all the trump cards. Bianca had had no choice but to cave in to his demands, not that she had fought too hard. She was going to decamp to Tuscany because the threat of losing the family fortune to a greedy, gold-digging toy boy was far more imperative a calling than sticking around in America so that custody could be more fairly shared.

She would see Rosa for a fortnight during the summer holidays, for ten days over Easter and they would split Christmas—unless she tried bending the rules, at which point, Gabriel had told her, he would slam into her like a freight train.

All was good. All was fine. And this…

He stood up, strolled to the floor-to-ceiling panes of glass that fortified his office, turning it into a glasshouse, and looked down twenty storeys to the streets below, thin and pulsing like thread veins. *This* was reality. *This* was what he had trained himself to appreciate. *This* was his life blood.

He and Izzy were not going to share space indefinitely. That had never been an option. It was staggering enough that she had shared his bedroom at all. None of his mistresses ever had, nor had he ever been tempted to issue any invitations.

And yet…

She was gone but she still filled his head. She'd left his bed and yet he still reached for her in the morning when he opened his eyes. Everywhere felt silent without her laughter filling the space between them. He closed his eyes and saw her face and his heart ached.

Forget about reality and bubbles that had to burst… Forget about pride and not having to justify himself to anyone. He hadn't been ready to let her go and, sitting here now, he finally admitted what he'd subconsciously been thinking for so long…

He might never be able to let her go.

Izzy sat back on her haunches and gazed at the mural she was in the process of creating. It was stiflingly hot inside the first of the cabanas to have been fully built based on the ideas she had had for the hotel, ideas which Max had put into place, as he had said he would.

Air conditioning was due to be installed when the remaining cabanas were all constructed, which would not be for another three months. Until then, she would work away in the heat, taking time out every so often to step outside and grab what little breeze there was.

Izzy didn't mind. She welcomed the stifling discomfort. It was more bearable than her inner torment, which was with her all the time, from the very moment she opened her eyes to the moment she closed them.

In theory, life was looking very good for her on all other fronts bar the emotional one. Max was in London at the moment, but they had had the most rewarding week together before he'd left. They'd actually talked and listened to one another. He'd sat next to Mia, his arm slung casually over her shoulder. Izzy had never seen anyone so much in love and her heart had twisted because, against all odds, he was living the dream she wanted so desperately for herself.

But it didn't erase the fact that she hadn't heard a word from Gabriel. She had closed the door behind her nearly a fortnight ago, and with that, she had closed a door to him and to Rosa…closed a window that had begun to feel like a dream. She could almost believe none of it had ever happened were it not for her memories, which were as sharp and as cruel as shards of glass inside her.

She was relying heavily on the cliché that time healed all.

Her mind was a million miles away, so when she heard *his* voice behind her, she didn't register that anyone had spoken at all until, a little louder, the voice said, 'I like it. Could I commission you to paint one for me?'

Very slowly, Izzy stood up and turned around.

Her heart was racing and, even as her brain recognised that distinctive deep, dark drawl, her impulse was to deny the obvious.

Her memory hadn't done him justice. He was even more devastatingly drop-dead gorgeous than she remembered. He wore cool, grey linen trousers, loafers, a faded grey polo-shirt… He looked urbane and elegant—as though the temperature wasn't in the high eighties.

While she was the opposite, with her short overalls daubed with paint, her hair tied up in something that was somewhat of a bun but not quite. Even her flip-flops had drops of paint on them. She was a mess.

'What are you doing here?'

'What do you think? I've come to see you.'

'Why?'

'Will you come with me so that we can talk? I have a chauffeur waiting outside.'

'What do we have to talk about, Gabriel?'

'Everything.'

'No. We don't.' She was furious because she could feel the prick of tears behind her eyes. Just looking at him opened up a well of sadness inside her. 'We're finished and it's much better if it's a clean break.'

'Is that what you want? A clean break?'

When she didn't answer, he looked away then strolled towards the mural, staring at it, his back to her.

'How do you think it felt for me to know that the stuff I'd said to you in confidence had gone into building a case against your ex?' Izzy asked, a wrenched accusation. 'You may think that's okay, because it was all for the sake of Rosa, but it didn't feel okay to me. I have *feelings*, and if you don't get that then forget it.'

'I hurt you.' He turned round to look at her, his movements for once lacking their usual assuredness.

'Yes. You did. And don't you *dare* tell me that there was anything cold or calculating about me sleeping with you because I was keen to help Evelyn. Don't even think of implying that it was some kind of trade off! It wasn't like that and it never could be. Not for me.'

'I know it wasn't.'

'And don't even think of trying to get me back into your bed again because you've decided you don't want a clean break.' She didn't want to look at him at all, but was still driven to stare, and she hated herself for her weakness.

'You're right,' Gabriel said huskily in a low, barely audible voice. 'I don't want a clean break. I don't want any break at all. I just…want you.'

'Too bad!' She spun round on her heels and half-raced out of the cabana. It was still scorching hot at a little after four and a combination of a need to flee and pure instinct drove her to run through the trees, brushing past the foliage that was in the process of being trimmed back, out past the main hotel and down towards the beach, which was empty.

He would follow her. She knew he would. She wanted it so badly, wanted *him* despite everything, and yet she was desperate to escape his stranglehold.

She didn't want him to talk her into doing anything her head would say no to and she feared her own weakness when it came to him.

She stopped dead to stare at the open ocean for a few seconds, to feel the soothing caress of the sea breeze cooling her down. Then she sat on the sand, drew up her knees to her chin and continued to look out at the deep-blue water with its white lacy spume where the waves rose and broke in a jagged pattern.

She felt his presence, saw his shadow over her and tensed up as he sat next to her, staring out, his body language mirroring hers.

'I didn't…use you,' he said haltingly, not looking at her. 'I just wasn't open. You talked, I listened and, instead of telling you how much you were doing to help me do the best for my daughter, I kept silent, because silence has always been my best friend. Rosa took to you, confided in you. I'd always promised that I would never put her in the middle, never make her feel as though she was taking sides in a situation not of her making. But she chatted to you and, instead of being honest with you, I wasn't. I should have trusted you. I should have communicated better but I just didn't have those skills. At least, I didn't think I did.'

'I hate you,' Izzy whispered. She brushed a tear off her cheek and was barely aware of doing so.

'This is who I am,' he said huskily. 'I grew up on the wrong side of the tracks and it was ingrained in me that my strength was my ability to remain focused. I think…' He sighed. 'I think when my marriage fell apart I woke up to the reality that love, and everything else that went with it, wasn't something I was capable of experiencing. Those were things sacrificed somewhere along the line. It was a sacrifice I accepted. I had my daughter. It was enough. And then you came along.'

'Don't do this. Don't lie to me.'

'I wouldn't. I couldn't.' He paused and Izzy sneaked a glance at him to find that he was staring off in the distance, as thoughtful as she had ever seen him.

'I slept with you that very first time, and if only I'd known just how much the foundations of my life would change afterwards… No, scratch that. I *met* you that very first time—so different from anyone I'd ever known. God, I told myself that you were just another privileged kid, that underneath the sweet and innocent veneer lay someone who would be accustomed to getting just want she wanted. On every count, I was wrong.'

He turned to her and looked at her gravely. 'That's why I couldn't use you although, yes, for better or for worse, I did use the information that came my way. I never asked you to confide in me…but you did, and

I was grateful because, in a strange way, you gave me my daughter. I don't want you to feel you have to forgive me, Izzy. I just want you to know that I fell in love with you and, if I hurt you, then from now to the end of time you have my apologies.'

He didn't touch her but their eyes met and the breath hitched in her throat.

Was he leading her up the garden path? This was a man who had just admitted that he was more than capable of using someone, that he had considered using her. Was this a ruse, something introduced to get her off-guard? Was there something else he wanted from her?

She didn't want to trust him but she could feel a singing in her veins.

'You're not in love with me,' she said, confused.

'I am. It's not something I ever expected, and I guess that's why I didn't recognise the signs. You shared my bed and I couldn't conceive of anything else. I trusted you with Rosa…let you open my eyes to what it felt like to stop being a businessman and instead to be just a dad. But trust was something that was so alien to me that I couldn't easily believe in it.'

'You never said before… You never let me know…'

'It crept up on me, Izzy. Like I said, I showed all the symptoms but chose to ignore them.' He reached to stroke the side of her face with his finger. She shivered and closed her eyes briefly.

'I don't want to believe you,' she said honestly and he smiled.

'Why not?'

'Because then I might wake up and realise that this has all been a dream.' She knew what it felt like to be giddy with happiness. 'I fell in love with you and I was so scared that it would all fall apart. I trusted Jefferson and that was a train crash. Did I dare trust you? Trust myself? If only I'd known how you felt then I might have been brave enough to tell you how *I* felt…'

'Or,' he said with wry honesty, 'You might have hit a brick wall. I closed myself off after Bianca and that detachment became my default position when it came to women. I figured it worked for me, gave me the uncluttered life I wanted. I didn't stop to ask myself what was lost in the process, but in the end you showed me.'

'I love you so much…' Her eyes shone. Nothing else mattered. This very moment was something to be held close and treasured, no more questions asked.

'I came here, Izzy, to ask you to marry me. I wanted to bring a ring…wanted to do something dramatic…but I was scared stiff that you'd turn me down. And if you turn me down, I'm not sure what I'll do. The truth is that it's more than love—it's need as well. I've spent my life insulating myself against the background I came from. I equated power and money with freedom and self-determination, and between those opposite poles there was nothing. Life, before you came along, was black and white. You turned it to Technicolor and that's why I want you by my side for ever. So will you, Izzy? Will you marry me?'

Izzy smiled and said two words to last a lifetime. 'I will.'

* * * * *

Captivated by
Promoted to the Italian's Fiancée*?*
You'll love the first instalment in the
Secrets of the Stowe Family trilogy
Forbidden Hawaiian Nights

And find your next page-turner with these
other stories by Cathy Williams!

The Italian's Christmas Proposition
His Secretary's Nine-Month Notice
Expecting His Billion-Dollar Scandal
The Forbidden Cabrera Brother

All available now

**WE HOPE YOU ENJOYED
THIS BOOK FROM**

HARLEQUIN

PRESENTS

Escape to exotic locations where passion knows no bounds.

Welcome to the glamorous lives of royals and billionaires,
where passion knows no bounds. Be swept into a world
of luxury, wealth and exotic locations.

8 NEW BOOKS AVAILABLE EVERY MONTH!

Love Harlequin romance?

DISCOVER.

Be the first to find out about promotions, news and exclusive content!

Facebook.com/HarlequinBooks

Twitter.com/HarlequinBooks

Instagram.com/HarlequinBooks

Pinterest.com/HarlequinBooks

YouTube.com/HarlequinBooks

ReaderService.com

EXPLORE.

Sign up for the Harlequin e-newsletter and download a free book from any series at **TryHarlequin.com**

CONNECT.

Join our Harlequin community to share your thoughts and connect with other romance readers!
Facebook.com/groups/HarlequinConnection